The Witch's Pet

Kendl Porter

Contents

1. Moonlit Resentment — 1

2. Enchanted Encounter — 4

3. Whispers of Darkness — 8

4. Torn By Tradition — 14

5. A Strong Bond — 20

6. A Witching Hour — 26

7. Trials and Tribulations — 34

8. A Witch's Song — 40

9. The Journey Begins — 53

10. Shadows of the Soul — 61

11. World Unknown — 69

12. Mending Deals — 77

13. Forging Alliances — 92

14. Fire and Water — 108

15. Shadows Dancing — 122

Moonlit Resentment

Dark clouds loomed overhead, casting an eerie shadow over the dense forest. Tyler stood at the edge of the pack, his golden eyes filled with a mixture of anger and frustration. The moonlight filtered through the canopy above, illuminating his meek frame and the fur bristling along his back. Ever since he could remember, Tyler had never quite fit in, never truly belonged. Born to be a leader among beasts, but could never meet the expectations and he resented every ounce of his heritage—his father's legacy. And yet, here he stood, torn between two worlds, longing for acceptance in either.

As the wind rustled through the leaves, carrying with it whispers of judgment and disdain, Tyler clenched his fists. The distant howl of his pack echoed in his ears—an affirmation of unity that felt more like a prison. Just a mile away, the flickering lights of the pack's gathering place beckoned, but he felt too raw to join them tonight. The weight of his father's legacy pressed down like a heavy cloak, suffocating and all too familiar. The further he distanced himself from the pack, the more he yearned for something wholly different—a place where he could be more than a wolf, more than an heir, where love might just break through the barriers his heritage had built.

Unbeknownst to Tyler, beneath the shadows of the trees, someone was watching. Tristian Lock lingered just out of sight, his heart racing with a mix of excitement and trepidation. The coven had always looked down on him, a mere male in a world of powerful witches, yet here he felt an undeniable pull towards the tortured wolf standing alone. Tristian had heard tales of a werewolf with a fractured spirit, one who could harness the power of the moon for his own bidding. But as he caught sight of Tyler's shimmering fur and the pain etched across his delicate features, a flicker of doubt crossed Tristian's mind. Could he truly exploit such vulnerability for his own gain, or had fate intertwined their paths for another purpose altogether?

Tristian carefully stepped back into the woods knowing that their fates would soon meet again, that is of course if everything went to plan.

The night deepened, swirling with an enchanting heaviness that made the air crackle with latent magic. Tyler turned away from the echoing howls of his pack, allowing the distant calls to wash over him like a haunting melody—a reminder of everything he could never be. He wandered deeper into the forest, needing space to breathe and contemplate, but there was something different tonight. The night felt alive, almost pulsating with an energy he couldn't quite place. A shiver skittered down his spine as he caught the faintest trace of a scent that was foreign yet enticing, something sweet mixed with earthy undertones.

Feeling an unexplainable urge, Tyler paused, looking around the endless shadows. "Is someone there?" he challenged into the darkness, his voice steady yet tinged with an undertone of vulnerability. The forest remained silent, but he didn't move. Instead, he listened intently, almost as if the very landscape itself was holding its breath.

The night stayed silent as the wolf looked around. It wasn't long before he could feel the tug of his pack bond try and draw the beta out...Tyler groaned a low growl before nodding and back towards the pack, thinking of that spell binding scent.

Enchanted Encounter

The bell above the entrance rang delicately as Tyler pushed open the ornate wooden door of Avalon's Enchantments—a doorway to a world he had never fully understood or was even supposed to like. The air was thick with an intoxicating mix of incense and ancient magic, drawing him further into its depths. Shelves lined with potion vials and mystical artifacts beckoned him closer, whispering secrets only known by witches and wizards. And amidst this realm of hidden wonders stood Tristian Lock—pale skin shimmering under the dim glow of enchanted candles, emerald eyes glinting mischievously behind thin-framed glasses. In that moment, Tyler felt an inexplicable pull towards this mysterious stranger that ignited a spark within him.

Tristian's eyes locked eyes on Tyler, saying nothing as he had the other night. Tristian watched the mutt closer as he walked around, his face unsure of anything in the store. Tyler looked at different colored candles and smelled every herb, taking note of every ingredient with his hyper senses.

"Uh, looking for something specific?" Tristian asked, breaking the silence as he stepped closer, his voice smooth and inviting.

Tyler turned abruptly, his golden eyes wide with surprise. "No, not really. Just... exploring." He glanced back at a shelf filled with shimmering crystals, now faking interest. "I didn't know magic shops had so much... stuff."

"There's more to magic than most realize," Tristian replied, a sly smile creeping across his lips. "It's not just spells and potions; it's about understanding the essence of every being."

Tyler raised an eyebrow, his frustration bubbling just beneath the surface. "And you think you understand that essence better than anyone else?" He crossed his arms defensively.

"Perhaps not better, but differently." Tristian took a step closer, intrigued by Tyler's fiery spirit. "What if I told you that the essence of a werewolf is more powerful than you think? Especially one like you."

"You know nothing about me," Tyler snapped, his heart racing for reasons he couldn't quite understand.

"Then let me learn." Tristian's gaze softened, earnest. "I can see it in your eyes. You're not just another wolf; there's something more. Something... conflicted."

Tyler's expression hardened. "You think I want to be some kind of experiment for you? I'm not just a magical curiosity."

Tristian frowned- only sarcastically, sensing Tyler's vulnerability beneath the bravado.

"Well then I suppose you should go back to your wolf pack mutt, because you clearly don't belong here." Tristan said with a long grin looking down at the 5'5 brown haired wolf boy.

Tyler's face flushed with anger, the repressed wolf inside him stirring at Tristian's taunt. "You don't know anything about me," he spat, the challenge hanging thick in the air. In that moment, the distance between them felt electric, charged with a tension he couldn't name. Yet, beneath the fury, a sliver of intrigue lingered—Tristian had seen through his defenses, grasping a vulnerability he had buried deep for years.

"Try me," Tristian replied, his tone shifting dramatically; it held a hint of earnestness now, a glimmer of curiosity that beckoned Tyler to let down his barriers. "Or maybe you need someone who can actually see you, beyond the alpha's son and spoiled pack.." Trisitian trailed off as he got slightly closer to the boy.

"How did you... who are you?" Tyler asked, looking up at Tristian and his silver short hair that faded to the black of his roots.

"What do you mean, who am I?" Tristian smirked, tilting his head slightly. "You walked into our coven's magic shop—don't you think that gives me some right to be curious? And my name is Tristian.. Tristian Lock" he gritted

Tyler narrowed his eyes, skepticism etched across his features. " Regardless, I didn't come here looking for a personal assistant, witch."

"Then it's a fortunate coincidence that I'm not at your service," Tristian replied, crossing his arms. "But let's be honest: you're here because you're searching for something. Am I right?"

Tyler hesitated, the heat of frustration cooling just a bit. "Maybe I am. But that doesn't mean I want guidance from a—" he paused, the word 'witch' lingering uncomfortably on his tongue, "—from you."

Tristian stepped closer, his emerald gaze unwavering. "You fear your duality, Tyler. The wolf and the boy—conflicting parts of you that yearn for acceptance. I see through your stuggles."

Tyler's heart raced. "You don't know me," he insisted, but his voice lacked conviction. "You can't—"

"Can't what? Can't possibly perceive the pain behind your fierce facade?" Tristian interjected, his voice barely above a whisper. "The desperation to break free? The loneliness of feeling out of place?"

Tyler's defiance faltered, a crack forming in his carefully constructed wall. Tristian's heart longed to keep talking but it was too soon to be too close.

"Go home Tyler"." Tristians voice rang but it almost echoed as his eyes glowed a faint mystic blue. Tyler's eyes went almost lifeless as if there was no one there at all.

"I think I should go home.." Tyler said quietly in his soft voice that made Tristian smirk with arrogance. Tyler slowly turned around away from Trisitian and walked out the door with the ring of the bell on the door being the last sound between them.

Whispers of Darkness

Tyler got to the front of his house before blinking and looking up. "What the.." Tyler started as he looked around wondering how he got back to the pack house without remembering anything. Tyler groaned realizing that he must have been hexed. Tyler cursed himself as well as witches as he turned around to go find the man who called himself Tristian. Tyler could feel his anger. He was always used as a pawn in other peoples games and he refused to be a part of another game even if his heart somehow felt differently towards the seemingly handsome witch.Tyler shook the last thought from his mind and replaced it with the original anger as he walked towards the lining of the woods before he heard the bushes rustle. His heart quicked as he looked towards the bushes and made out a tall masculine figure, it was Bruce Baxer. He wasn't the only figure that threw a large shadow onto the ground. Bruce was followed by: Dylan, Austin, and Seth Torris... the worst but strongest brothers that the pack had to offer."Where have you been mutt?" Bruce asked in a vile tone. "We were almost starting to miss you." he lied as he turned around the three brothers he called his friends who were now egging Bruce on.Tyler swallowed hard, feeling the familiar sting of resentment wash over him. "I didn't realize I needed to check in with you, Bruce.""Oh, but you do," Bruce replied, stepping closer, his muscular frame looming over Tyler. "You're still part of this pack, whether you want to be or not."Dylan chuckled, positioning himself to block any retreat. "What's the matter, pup? Afraid of confronting your true self?"Tyler narrowed his eyes, his body tensing with every taunt. "I know who I am. You feral beast wouldn't understand."Seth took a step forward, smirking. "That's rich coming from you. Hiding in the woods like a lost little wolf. Your nickname could be 'the Ghost of Baxtrail.'"Tyler's fists clenched, the urge to retaliate bubbling inside him. "At least I don't bow before the alpha like you fools."Austin laughed, crossing his arms. "Is that what this is about? Your father?" He leaned in, voice dripping with mockery. "Is it that you're tired of living in his shadow, or are you just mad because you can't be the alpha?""Shut up!" Tyler shot back, taking a step forward, fury igniting in his golden eyes."Well, well, someone's feisty tonight," Bruce taunted, enjoying the reaction. "how about we put that fight to the test?" Bruce asked as he taunted Tyler.Tyler's heartbeat thundered in his ears, adrenaline racing through him as he faced the four-pack bullies. His instincts screamed at him to run, to retreat back into the safety of the woods, but the anger bubbling inside wouldn't let him yield. "You really think you can take me on, Bruce? Because I'm more than just your 'mutt,'" Tyler growled, his voice low and fierce, daring Bruce to make a move.The glint in Bruce's eyes shifted to something more predatory. "How about a little showdown? Just you and me. Show everyone here who really belongs in this pack." He motioned to the brothers who chuckled, their laughter a chorus of cruelty that sliced into Tyler's resolve. He could feel the stakes being laid bare beneath the flickering starlight, a challenge that called to the wolf instinct nestled deep within him.Bruce smiled and the brothers surrounded them so that there was the rough shape of a ring. Tyler lunged at Bruce but Bruce was quick, slamming the smaller wolf to the ground.Tyler's body hit the ground with a harsh thud, the breath pushed out of him. Stars erupted in his vision, and for a moment, he lay there dazed and vulnerable beneath Bruce's weight. The laughter of the brothers echoed around him, but within the chaos, Tyler felt a spark of defiance ignite in his gut. "You think this makes you stronger?" he hissed, struggling against Bruce's grip. "You're nothing but a coward hiding behind your pack."Bruce's expression darkened, eyes flickering with irritation. "Coward? Is that what you call the one who puts you in your place? You talk big for someone who's all bark and no bite." He shoved Tyler's face into the dirt, pressing down with his weight."I'll show you who owns you mutt." Bruce started to undo his pants with one hand as he laid on top of Tyler keeping him down. The brothers looked at each other knowing this was wrong but refusing to disobey Bruce. "I'll show you what bad and weak wolves get," Bruce finished as he went to undo Tylers pants.The air was thick with tension, the laughter of the brothers fading into an uneasy silence. Tyler's heart raced, a primal instinct surging within him that had nothing to do with fear. With a sudden burst of strength, he clawed his way out from beneath Bruce, desperate to break free from the humiliation that suffocated him. "You don't know anything about me," Tyler spat, his voice low yet filled with fierce defiance as he rose to his feet, a mix of anger and adrenaline coursing through his veins.But before Tyler could make a definitive move, a sharp crack echoed through the clearing, drawing the attention of the pack. Emerging from the shadows, a figure stepped into the ring formed by the brothers. Tristian Lock, the male witch, pierced the scene with his probing gaze. His voluminous cloak swayed dramatically, giving him an air of authority that momentarily distracted even the fiercest of wolves. "What a spectacle," he remarked dryly, an amused glint in his emerald eyes. "Is this how your pack fosters strength? By bullying those who refuse to submit?"Bruce's eyes narrowed, irritation flickering across his face, but he hesitated, uncertainty creeping in as he processed the witch's presence. The other brothers exchanged glances, unsure whom they should side with now, a witch being a strange intervention no one anticipated. Tristian stepped closer, the aura around him alive with latent power. "Fight me instead, Bruce," he challenged, the weight of the words pulling the air tight.

"Show me how strong you truly are."Tyler stared at Tristian, bewildered but desperate for an ally, a lifeline against the pack's cruelty. It was madness, yet Tyler felt something shift within him—an unfamiliar flutter of hope. Maybe, just maybe, he didn't have to face this alone. As his eyes locked with Tristian's, Tyler sensed a bond forming, one that would either strengthen them both or plunge them deeper into the darkness looming just beyond the edges of the clearing.Tristian's emerald eyes flickered between Tyler and Bruce, a smirk playing on his lips. "Or are you afraid of a little competition?" he taunted, stepping forward, his presence commanding the attention of the gathered wolves.Bruce tilted his head, his arrogance mingling with uncertainty. "You think you can take me on? You're all talk, witch.""I'm more than just talk," Tristian replied, his voice smooth yet edged with a challenge. "You clearly don't understand the kind of magic I'm capable of."Tyler felt a surge of admiration for Tristian in that moment, though he also felt a knot of apprehension. "You can't just... come in here and—""Watch me," Tristian interrupted, his confidence unwavering. He faced Bruce, folding his arms. "Let's see if your strength is matched by your skill. Or will you crumble like the bully you are?"Austin scoffed, moving to the side. "This is madness. You're going to regret this, Lock!""Yes, let's see how this unfolds," Bruce spat, his confidence re-emerging as he stepped closer to Tristian, his eyes narrowing. "Bring it on, you wannabe sorcerer ."Before Bruce could react, Tristian lifted his hands, murmuring incantations under his breath. A shimmering barrier encased him, forcing Bruce to stumble back, both surprise and anger flashing across his face.The crackling energy enveloped Tristian, swirling like a vibrant storm around him, a visual representation of his determination. He felt the power coursing through his veins, a sensation that sparked both excitement and fear. "You think your jaw muscles are enough to handle real magic?" he taunted, his voice steady as he maintained eye contact with Bruce. Just beyond the barrier, the pack watched with bated breath, unable to ignore the palpable confrontation unfolding before them.Bruce's expression morphed from anger to incredulity as he grappled with the strange sensation of vulnerability.

"What the hell is this? Sorcery won't save you!" He lunged, baring his teeth, the feral gleam in his eyes revealing both panic and pride. Yet as he collided with the barrier, the force pushed him back effortlessly, knocking him off balance. The pack brothers murmurs filled the clearing, uncertainty now weaving through their ranks like an intoxicating fragrance. "Watch closely, wolves," Tristian called out, his voice dripping with disdain. "This is real strength." He gestured sharply with his hands, and the air thickened with energy, pulling at their senses. Tendrils of magic lashed out, shimmering with potential and intent, swirling towards Bruce as if they were extensions of his will. "This isn't just a show—it's a lesson." While Tyler stood frozen, caught in the whirlpool of his emotions, he felt the weight of potential alliances forming. Tristian may have arrived as a savior, but it was clear he had his own ambitions, one that could ensnare Tyler in a web of magic and desire. Would he dare to embrace the chaos and forge a bond, or would he run back to the safety of his wounded pride? The moment hung heavy, teetering on the edge of destiny. "Stop"." The words came surprisingly from Tylers own mouth. "This is stupid and is just gonna make things worse. He said, trying not to stumble over his own words. Tristian's green gaze flickered toward Tyler, confusion mingling with surprise. "Are you serious?" he asked, his voice low but intense. "You want to give in to them? After everything?" Tyler's fists clenched, but he straightened up, shaking off the weight of uncertainty that cloaked him. "No, I don't want to give in! But I won't stand by and let this escalate into something we can't control." Bruce scoffed, rolling his eyes with a smirk. "Look at Mr. Rebellious trying to play the hero. It's cute." Dylan piped up, "Did your precious witch spin a spell to help you find your backbone?" Tyler turned toward them, his heart racing. "This isn't about you, Bruce," he shot back. "This is about me taking control for once." Tristian stepped closer, intrigued. "Then take control, Tyler. Don't let them demean you like this." "I won't let them! But I won't let you make things worse either, Tristian." Tyler's voice was steadier now, filled with defiance. "If you honestly care about me, you should walk away." Bruce laughed mockingly. "And go back to sulking in your daddy's shadow? No way!""Shut it, Bruce!" Tyler snapped, a growl creeping into his voice. "You think you can dictate my choices? Not anymore. With that Tristian sighed and nodded, "as you wish..pet " he finished as he vanished into thin air.The brothers exchanged glances before looking at Bruce... "We should all go man.. leave him." Seth piped up. Bruce nodded before giving Tyler one last grueling stare before turning away. Tyler stood there for a minute waiting for them to leave before he let his tears fall to the ground.'Pet' rang in his mind as his tears fell. The word made him feel small and weak but coming from Tristian, the way his voice said them, almost not asking but telling him. Tyler wiped his eyes as he bit his lip."Pet"

Torn By Tradition

T he Great Hall illuminated with blinding daylight as Tyler walked on the perfectly polished wooden floors. The Baxtrail pack had just joined for breakfast together as they did daily around 7:00 A.M. Tyler strolled down the nearly empty aisle between tables. As he passed each table the pack got quiet one by one. Tyler tried not to notice, resenting the fear that rumor had spread about the altercation, Tyler being made out to be the villain no doubt. Tyler strolled on trying to keep his head held high as he finally met his fathers lingering eyes.

The moment Tyler locked eyes with his father, the atmosphere shifted like a storm brewing over an otherwise calm sea. Alpha Marcus Lune's gaze was stern, betraying the whirlwind of emotions swirling within—concern, disappointment, and a hint of pride flickered behind the mask of authority. Tyler felt every beat of silence intensify as the pack members whispered among themselves, casting furtive glances, each one an echo of his struggles. It was as if he carried the weight of their judgment on his shoulders, and yet, an ember of defiance sparked within him.

"Tyler," his father finally spoke, his voice resonating through the hall like a bell tolling at dawn. "We need to talk about what happened yesterday." The pack turned their attention toward him, each breath held in anticipation of a looming confrontation. Deep inside, Tyler felt the urge to flee, but the swell of his newfound resolve thwarted any attempt at retreat. This was his moment.

"In front of everyone?" Tyler asked, forcing a tone of indifference that barely masked his anxiety. "Might as well make it a spectacle, right?" The words dripped with defiance, and he could feel the murmurs around him swell into a tide of tension.

"Right because it's always better to put me in my place in front of everyone, right?" Tyler asked, his voice meek and tired.

"What did you just say to me boy?" Alpha Marcus asked, his voice becoming more stern towards the boy.

Tyler felt the heat of his father's gaze like fire on his skin, a mix of anger and hurt flooding his chest. "I said, it always seems to come down to you putting me in my place," Tyler replied, trying hard to keep his voice steady. "Not even a moment's thought about how I feel."

"Do you think this is easy for me?" Marcus's voice rose slightly, causing some pack members to shift uneasily in their seats. "This isn't just about you, Tyler. It's about the pack!"

"About the pack?" Tyler scoffed, frustration bubbling beneath the surface. "All I see is a bunch of wolves waiting for a chance to tear me apart the moment I step out of line. I'm sick of it!"

"Enough!" Marcus commanded, his authoritative tone cutting through the murmurs rippling through the hall. "You will respect the traditions of this pack, and you will adhere to the rules!"

"Rules?" Tyler asked as he almost huffed, everyone's eyes certainly on the spectacle at this point.

"Where were the rules when Bruce..." Tyler began before he trailed off.

"Where were the rules when Bruce was attacking me?" Tyler finished, his heart pounding in his chest. "Rules don't protect me; they only serve to keep me beneath your thumb."

"Watch your tone," Marcus warned, leaning forward, a scowl etched across his features. "This rebellion serves no one. You need to understand your role."

"My role?" Tyler echoed incredulously, his voice rising with the weight of his frustration. "I'm not a pawn in your game. I'm tired of being defined by your expectations!"

The hall erupted in whispers, the tension thickening with every word exchanged. A few members looked unsure, exchanging nervous glances, while most seemed to relish the drama unfolding.

"Is this what you want, Tyler?" Marcus pressed, his voice softer this time but still holding authority. "To fight against your own family?"

"It's not just about family anymore!" Tyler shouted, anger coursing through him. "It's about me finding my own place, free of your constraints and the pack's judgment. You don't know what it's like to be suffocated by tradition!"

"I know what it means to carry responsibility," Marcus snapped back, his patience wearing thin. "You aren't alone in this. The pack thrives on unity; your actions have consequences that extend far beyond just you."

"Consequences?" Tyler felt the bitterness rising within him. "The only consequence I see is the suffocation of my true self.

At this point the alpha's eyes were glowing a dark shade most would never want to encounter.

"Tyler you are pushing your luck and I advise that you back down now...
son" Marcus said the last part with disdain, as if he were looking at a
stranger.

A tense silence enveloped the room, broken only by the soft rustle of fur
as pack members bristled in response to the brewing storm. Tyler's heart
raced, a dissonant symphony of anger and fear strumming at his nerves.
The words hung heavy in the air: "Back down now... son." It felt as if
Marcus had drawn an invisible line, one that cast Tyler further into the
shadows of rebellion. He clenched his fists, nails digging into his palms,
sensing the bittersweet thrill of defiance mingling with the ache of familial
ties fraying beneath the strain.

Before he could respond, a shiver ran down his spine, right there, at the
threshold where the polished wooden door met the glow of the gathering
storm outside. A gust of wind swept through the hall, rustling the fur of
the wolves and extinguishing a couple of candles along the wall. From the
swirling shadows emerged a figure, wiry and ethereal—Tristian Lock, with
his unruly hair and cloak that billowed like secrets woven into the night.
His presence shifted the atmosphere, pulling Tyler's attention from his
father as if by some unseen magic.

"Ah, the mighty Alpha and his wayward son," Tristian spoke, voice low and
smooth, threading through the tension with a seductive drawl. "Fighting
over tradition like children arguing over a broken toy." His eyes gleamed
with mischief, but beneath the surface, Tyler sensed an empathy—an understanding of feeling out of place. "Perhaps what's needed here isn't more
rules but a little of that so-called chaos." The witch stepped further into
the hall, an unsettling light spilling around him as though he carried the
twilight within. "I can show you how to break free from what binds you,
Tyler. All it takes is a touch of magic."

Tyler felt a twitch of intrigue at Tristian's words, a flicker of hope mingling with the defiance boiling within. Would he dare step toward this strange ally, a potential avenue for liberation?

"What is this?" Marcus shouted. The pack surrounded them quickly, growling in defense as they watched the witch closely In Front of them.

"We do not accept witches here" The Alpha exclaimed as he stared Tristian in the eyes

Tyler's pulse quickened as he faced the conflict of his life. The whispers of the pack turned to growls, their anger palpable, and it felt as though the very air around them crackled with tension. Yet, standing beside Tristian, he felt a curious spark of exhilaration. "What if I want to accept him?" Tyler challenged, glancing at Marcus with defiance as fierce as a summer storm. "I'm tired of living beneath the weight of your rules, and this—" he swept his hand in Tristian's direction, "—might be the key to my freedom!"

Marcus's eyes flared with disbelief, a fierce storm brewing beneath his vigilant façade. "You would side with a witch? A male witch at that? Think of the consequences, Tyler!" His voice reverberated through the hall like thunder, but for the first time, Tyler felt something other than fear in the face of his father's wrath: resolve.

"It's not about sides anymore, Dad," Tyler spat the words, breaths ragged yet fervent. "I'm choosing my own path, with or without your approval." The tension thickened as the pack members shifted uncertainly, glancing between their agitated Alpha and the boy they'd always seen as less than. But Tyler was reclaiming his truth, a truth he felt echoed in Tristian's shadowy presence. Their eyes met—something beyond mere circumstance tethered them together in this tumultuous moment.

"Very well," Tristian said, his voice cool yet conspiratorial, piercing through the chaos. He stepped closer, the moonlight catching the glint of a small charm dangling from his neck. "If you're serious about wanting a life unfettered by tradition, let me guide you. Together, we could wield chaos as a weapon—or a tool for rebirth. The choice is yours, Tyler. Are you ready to embrace your true self?"

Before he could think too long, Tyler nodded, the defiance igniting a fire within. This was his chance—to cast away the shadow of expectation and step into the light of something uniquely his own. He turned back toward Marcus, seeing the betrayal transforming into a mix of fear and rage—the unmistakable signs of a father losing control of his son.

"Alpha Marcus, I do give my condolences." Tristian said with a smug smile.

Marcus growled loudly as his fingernails extended as well as his k-9's

"Hold on tight mutt." was the last thing Tristian said before they were whisked away in a swirl of air and smoke.

A Strong Bond

They landed with a thud against the ground, the fresh scent of pine mingling with the sharp tang of ozone. Tyler blinked, dazed by the sudden shift from the oppressive atmosphere of his father's pack to the serene solitude of a nearby clearing. The moon hung low, framing Tristian in ethereal light, his expression a mix of triumph and delight, but there was something dangerously alluring in his eyes that sent a jolt through Tyler's system.

"Welcome to my world—or what few would dare let it be..," Tristian started before trailing off.

The sound of vomiting rang through the woods of North Carolina as Tyler spewed his guts.

"It'll be okay, you'll get used to teleporting." Tristian replied, trying not to laugh at poor Tyler, looking as green as the leaves he was now puking on.

"I don't think that i'll ever get used to that." he retorted as he wiped his mouth with the back of his forearm.

"Next time, maybe a warning before you just... whisk me away?" Tyler managed, his voice still shaky as he leaned against a nearby tree for support.

Tristian chuckled softly, his emerald eyes sparkling with mischief. "Oh, but where's the fun in that? You've got to embrace the chaos, Tyler."

"Embrace the chaos?" Tyler echoed incredulously. His stomach was finally settling, but the thought of what might be ahead made his heart race. "I'm not sure chaos is what I need right now."

"Believe me, it's exactly what you need," Tristian insisted, stepping closer. "Every great journey begins with a little discomfort. Besides, haven't you felt more alive since we met?"

A flicker of something warm shot through Tyler at those words, and he swallowed hard. "Yeah, but alive doesn't mean I should let a stranger me take me to an unknown location in the woods"-

"Where are we anyway?" he asked as he looked around, hearing the black crows caw.

"We're just outside my coven." Tristian said with spite in his tone.

Tyler straightened himself, brushing off the evidence of his earlier nausea. "Great, so we're in the land of the witches. Fantastic. How do I not get killed just by being here?"

Tristian leaned against a tree, crossing his arms with a smirk. "You think they would dare harm the Alpha's son? Besides, you're with me. Just focus on staying low. I don't plan on being here long anyway, we just have to get something."

Tyler raised an eyebrow, skepticism swirling in his chest. "So, you expect me to just trust you? You do realize you're still a total stranger, right?"

A shadow crossed Tristian's face as his tone turned more serious. "You may not know me fully, Tyler, but I promise I have your best interests at heart.

I plan to use this time to help you embrace your true self, not just for my own gain."

Tyler sighed, rubbing the back of his neck, feeling the weight of uncertainty. "I appreciate that, I really do. But you have to admit, it's a little difficult to trust someone when I've just been used and judged my whole life."

"You think I don't know about judgment?" Tristian shot back, eyes narrowing. "I've faced derision from my own coven simply for existing as a witch, just as you have with your pack. We're not so different, you and I."

Tyler met Tristian's gaze, the shared understanding weaving an unexpected bond between them. Tyler nodded looking at Tristan, something different in his eyes, hurt maybe? Tyler didn't know but it made him feel almost bad. Tyler could feel his wolf also feeling bad, almost as if his wolf was upset about Tristian's sadness and screamed to protect him.

"Look, I didn't mean to assume," Tyler said, his voice softening. "It's just... it's hard to wrap my head around all of this. You and I, we seem like opposites."

Tristian shrugged, a playful grin returning. "Opposites attract, right? Besides, deep down, I think you're ready to embrace who you really are—the wolf and whatever else lies beneath. You just need the right nudge."

Tyler chuckled, shaking his head. "A nudge? Is that what you call this whirlwind of chaos?"

"Pretty much," Tristian replied, crossing his arms with a self-satisfied smirk. "A necessary chaos to shake things up. Trust me, you'll thank me later."

"Yeah, I'll be sure to remember that when I'm facing down your witch friends," Tyler replied, rolling his eyes but unable to suppress a smile.

"They're not all bad, you know," Tristian said, his tone earnest. "They just need to understand you, just like everyone else. You have to show them who you are—fight against their expectations."

"And how do you expect me to do that?" Tyler challenged, eyebrows furrowed. "I mean, being the Alpha's son isn't exactly a great start. They'll never accept me."

Tristian stepped closer, his intensity piercing through Tyler's uncertainty. "But what if you redefine what it means to be that" Tristian finished.

Tyler nodded before looking Tyler directly in the eyes. "You still haven't told me how you are even going to show me more of my wolf side or even what that means.." Tyler said, looking at him with a raised eyebrow.

"Ah, there's the spark!" Tristian replied, his eyes lighting up. "Let's start with tapping into your instincts—your true nature. We must form a bond, Tyler. Magic thrives on connection."

"Connection?" Tyler echoed skeptically. "You mean like some kind of, what, witchy buddy system?"

"Precisely! You've got it," Tristian in one swoop grabbed Tyler pulling him close to his body with a large smirk.

"What are you doing?" Tyler asked in total shock.

"Well I think the best way to do that would be to kiss."- Tristian said he raised a seductive eyebrow. "It's a fast way to show trust and bond," he said, trying to reassure Tyler.

"I mean I guess we can.." he said with hesitation in his draw.

Tristian's smirk faded slightly as he studied Tyler's uncertain expression, searching for any hint of discomfort. Sensing the air between them thicken with tension, he leaned in closer, allowing a playful glint to return to his eyes. "Or we could skip to the part where I teach you to embrace your wolf side first," he suggested, his voice a soft murmur, teasing a smile back onto Tyler's lips.

Tyler inhaled deeply, the scent of moss and blooming wildflowers swirling into his senses, grounding him. For a heartbeat, he considered the chaos that could unfold with a single kiss that his wolf now ached for, and despite every warning bell ringing in his mind, he felt an undeniable tug within him. Maybe it was the wolf—itching for acknowledgement, a creature struggling against the confines of acceptance. "Alright then, show me what you've got."

Tristian's smile widened at Tyler's reluctant concession, his heart racing with anticipation. "Follow my lead," he urged softly, stepping back to give them both space. His fingers twitched with dormant magic, eager to flow through their connection. "This isn't just about a kiss. It's about awakening your instincts, your inner strength."

Tyler straightened, his posture shifting with rising adrenaline as he mirrored Tristian's intensity. "What do I have to do?" He was ready, even if the thought of standing before the fire of his own uncharted power made him uneasy.

"Let go of your fear, Tyler," Tristian instructed, his voice steady. "We're going to tap into your wolf. Breathe with me." He took a deep breath, his chest expanding, and Tyler followed suit, inhaling the earthy scent around them—age-old trees and wild blooms now filling every fiber of his being. "Now, picture your wolf—the wildness, the freedom. Take that image... and let it consume you."

As Tyler closed his eyes, he felt warmth spiraling inside him, a flutter that made his skin itch. With each breath, he imagined the sleek figure of his wolf, powerful and free, racing through the moonlit forest. He envisioned the moon's glow casting silver light upon soft fur, and a growl that resonated with the very core of him. "I can see it," he murmured, nerves melting into something exhilarating.

"Good," Tristian urged, his voice a low chant, intertwining with Tyler's thoughts. "Now, bring that essence back. Channel it into our bond." Their eyes met, and in that moment, a spark danced in the air—a connection forged in vulnerability and burgeoning trust.

"Okay," Tyler nodded, his heartbeat drumming wildly in tune with the rise of his instincts. He reached out, a tentative hand grasping Tristian's wrist. "Together?"

"Together," Tristian confirmed, a calm resolve settling between them, both reveling in the magic blossoming amidst shared breaths and unspoken promises. With a swift motion, Tristian leaned in, sealing their connection with a kiss that ignited a pulse of energy, a spark of raw potential that felt as natural as furning in the wild. Tyler moaned quietly, enjoying every second before the leaves started to rustle. The birds called out and flew from the trees as the clouds turned a dark gray with hues of green.

Tyler let go as they both looked up.'

"What's happening?" Tyler asked with fear in his voice.

"My mother.." Trisitian replied as they both locked eyes.

A Witching Hour

S uddenly, the atmosphere shifted, charged with an unsettling energy that seemed to crackle between them. The wind picked up, rustling the leaves of the ancient trees that surrounded the clearing, and the darkening clouds loomed ominously above them as if the sky itself had become an extension of Tristian's brewing magic. "We need to move," he said urgently, pulling Tyler close. "My mother has been searching for me. I should have sensed her, but I was too wrapped up in this...." he said looking into Tyler's eyes.

"Is she dangerous?" Tyler asked, the fear in his voice overshadowed by curiosity. His instincts screamed at him to run, to shift into his wolf form and sprint into the safety of the forest. But there was something about Tristian—the way his emerald eyes sparkled with a mix of worry and determination—that kept him rooted to the spot.

"Dangerous doesn't quite capture it," Tristian admitted, glancing around nervously as if expecting his mother to emerge from the shadows at any moment. "She's powerful, and she won't understand what we've just done. She believes magic is only for the witches of our coven—especially women. A bond like ours? That's taboo."

"I need you to hide." said sternly, commanding Tyler as he looked at the swirling clouds above them.

Tyler looked at Tristian with a confused look while simoustanly looking for a tree to hide behind. "What's so bad about about your mom?" Tyler asked as starting to move to a near tree. "I thought you said no one would kill me.." Tyler said looking back at Trisitan

"They won't be with me near you, but my mother is the head of the coven and she will want answers as to why I would even want to bring a wolf to our territory. It'll be better to let me handle her while she's angry. Now I need you to go hide!" Tristian replied with a stern and forceful tone.

The wind picked up, swirling around them with a sudden sharpness, as if echoing Tristian's urgency. Tyler's heart raced, a mixture of fear and confusion flooding his senses. "But I need to be here!" he protested, grounding himself as he caught the storm brewing in Tristian's dark eyes. "You shouldn't have to face her alone! What if she—"

"Tyler!" Tristian cut him off, his voice more urgent than ever. "If you don't hide, I'll never forgive myself if she sees you. Please, just trust me."

With a reluctant nod, Tyler turned away, his feet moving instinctively toward the thick brush at the edge of the clearing, but his heart remained planted beside Tristian. He ducked behind a towering oak, its gnarled roots clutching the earth like ancient guardians. From his concealed vantage, he could just make out Tristian's silhouette, a figure brimming with intent against the encroaching storm.

As Tristian stepped into the open, the clouds shifted ominously, dark tendrils weaving like mist around him. "Mother!" Tristian called out, his voice steady, yet laced with tension. "What brings you here?"

A figure emerged from the shadows of the trees, her presence commanding and suffused with raw magic. The air crackled with power at her approach, and Tyler felt a chill race down his spine. She was an ethereal beauty cloaked in flowing robes of midnight blue, her long silver hair cascading like moonlight around her shoulders. "You know why I'm here, son." Her voice was as smooth as silk, yet held a dangerous edge. "You dare to consort with a wolf?"

From his hiding place, Tyler gripped the trunk of the tree, fear knotting in his stomach as he waited, heart pounding, unsure whether to hope for Tristian's defiance or fear what his mother's wrath would unleash. The fate of their bond hung in the balance, precariously teetering on the edge of magic and tension.

"It's not what you think mother." Trisitan said softly. "I was just trying to make a friend and I met Tyler.." he finished hoping that his mother would buy his story.

Tristian's mother narrowed her eyes, assessing her son with an inscrutable gaze. "A friend? Or a pet? Are you really willing to risk our coven's reputation for the son of an Alpha wolf?"

"He's not a pet!" Tristian shot back, glancing toward Tyler's hiding place and hoping his expression of fire matched the anger curling in his own stomach. "He's—"

"—a wolf," she interrupted, her voice sharp like a crack of thunder. "You are playing a dangerous game, Tristian. You know how our coven feels about interspecies relationships. This isn't just a friendship; it's forbidden."

Tyler's heart sank at the word forbidden. He moved silently, straining to hear Tristian's response.

Tristian's mother stepped toward her son and reached her hand out and slowly caressed his cheek.

"My sweet boy... so loving and trusting. Why must you always go against the grain?" she asked, staring into Tristian's eyes.

"Because," Tristian said, his voice firm despite the tremor of emotion beneath it, "this is my choice. Tyler is more than just a wolf to me; he sees me for who I really am, not just a witch or a male among females."

"He's the Alpha's son!" she hissed, her disdain palpable. "You think the pack will allow this? You're inviting chaos into our lives, son!"

"Maybe chaos is what we need!" Tristian argued, stepping back defiantly. "I'm tired of playing by rules that strip me of who I am. Tyler deserves a chance to be free, just like I do."

"Free?" she scoffed, her lips curling into a sneer. "You've chosen a wolf, Tristian! You're not just challenging the coven; you're defying nature itself!"

"He's not just a wolf!" Tyler finally spoke, his heart racing. He stepped out from behind the tree, emboldened by Tristian's words. "I'm not some beast for you to dismiss! I'm more than what you've been told."

Tristian's mother turned, her expression darkening. "And you think that's enough? That you two can just waltz through life hand in hand without consequences?"

"Maybe you need to see past your prejudices," Tyler challenged.

"Silence mutt!" she said. In that moment Tyler's mouth forcefully closed, a magic that Tyler didn't even know existed.

Tristian's eyes widened in horror as he watched the spell weave like an invisible ribbon around Tyler's mouth, rendering him voiceless. Every fiber of his being screamed in protest, but he held his ground, glaring defiantly at his mother. "Let him speak!" he demanded, the authority in his voice surprising even him.

"And let him spread his taint on our lineage?" She stepped closer to Tyler, her presence suffocating, drawing in the shadows like a dark cloak around her form. "You have no idea the kind of danger you invite into our lives. Wolves and witches are not meant to intertwine, Tristian. You're blind to the chaos you seek!"

Tyler's mind raced, desperately trying to prop open the walls of the magic that held him captive. In that instant, he felt a thin strand of energy connecting him to Tristian—a glimmer of hope against the darkness. He could see it in Tristian's fierce brown eyes, a fire that nearly rivaled the elemental forces surrounding them, and he remembered what he was: a wolf, yes, but also a fighter.

"Time to look deeper," Tyler thought, pouring his strength into that fraying connection. "This isn't just about rules or prejudice. This is about love—something you could never understand!"

Suddenly, the magic binding him shuddered. With a surge of newfound will, Tyler pushed back, a forceful whisper slipping past the barrier of his mouth, "Tristian, I won't let her take me from you!" The words, though faint, carried a power that rippled through the air. Tristian caught the determined glint in Tyler's eyes, and for the first time since their meeting, he understood: this bond was a spell more potent than any magic his mother could conjure.

"Enough!" Tristian's mother shouted, her voice resonant with fury, but the cracks in her composure started to show. "You dare to challenge me?"

"Yes!" Tristian yelled, stepping forward, his heart thrumming with a combination of fear and hope.

"Tristian Lock you will stand trial for this treachery. You are my son and I love you but this will not go unpunished and you will explain yourself in front of us 13." His mother replied, her tongue sharp.

"13?" Tyler asked, looking at Tristan's eyes went wide.

"The witch Tribunal, you ignorant dog" His mother replied.

"They make sure all witch laws are followed.." Tristian said, looking towards Tyler, trying not to sound nervous.

"What happens at this Tribunal?" Tyler asked, his heart pounding in his chest. He could feel the shadows closing in, each moment bringing a new wave of anxiety.

Tristian turned, urgency etched in his features as he closed the distance between them. "It's... it's a trial," he explained, his voice strained. "The coven will decide whether our bond is an affront to nature or something worth embracing."

"Sounds pretty terrifying," Tyler replied, trying to keep his voice steady. "What if they don't understand? What if they side with your mother?"

"They might," Tristian admitted, his emerald eyes darkening with worry. "But I won't let them dictate who I care for, or who I love."

Tyler felt an unexpected warmth swell in his chest. "You'd really stand against your coven for me?"

"Absolutely," Tristian replied fiercely, grasping Tyler's hands. "What we have is worth fighting for. I believe in us, Tyler. I need you to believe too."

"I want to," Tyler replied, his voice barely above a whisper, "but it's hard to fight when I can't even speak." He glanced at Tristian's mother, her gaze now simmering with restrained fury.

The air hung heavy with tension, and Tristian's mother raised an eyebrow, crossing her arms. "Words are only smoke and mirrors, boy. You think your bond is some enchanted shield against reality and we will decide that fate for you." she finished as looked at both of the young men in front of her. "Enjoy your time while it lasts, you'll only have till midnight.

Her last words sent a chilling energy down both their spines. Tristian's mothers eyes glowed as the wind started swimming and leaves started groaning before she disappeared into the air.

Tyler's heart raced, a mix of fear and determination igniting a fire within him. Midnight loomed ahead like a dark cloud threatening to rain down disaster. Would the Tribunal see the truth of their connection, or would they allow archaic prejudice to drown out love? With Tristian's hands in his, Tyler felt an electricity pulsate beyond their grips—a promise, a flicker of hope in the encroaching shadows.

"We can't waste time," Tyler said, his voice steadier than he felt. "We need to prepare. What if we practiced a spell to strengthen our bond? If we truly believe, maybe it can turn the Tribunal's judgment in our favor."

Tristian absorbed his suggestion, the power of it coursing through his veins. "I can teach you how to harness your energy, how to amplify it. If we produce a display of our connection, it might just sway them." His eyes shone bright with determination, rallying against the weight of their circumstances. "But there's no guaranteeing it would work."

Tristian looked around the woods. The feeling had shifted, almost as if now they were being watched.

"We will have to do a spell...and you aren't trained in magic Tyler..." Tristian spoke with fear and questionability.

"I might have an idea but you'll just have to go with me on it, unfortunately it's only something that can happen once we are there.... and it involves singing.. kinda."

"Singing"? Tyler asked, confused.

"There is magic in notes and song...there's an old practice among witches to prove bonds between each other. It was used in a time where a witch wanted to get married against the will of her father. The ritual was used to prove true connection ...." Tristian responded.

"Are you serious?" Tyler asked, a mix of surprise and disbelief in his eyes. "You actually want me to sing?"

"Yes," Tristian insisted, a determined glint in his emerald eyes. "Think of it as a spell. We've just got to channel our energy into the melody, amplifying our bond. If we do it right, we could show them just how strong we are together."

Tyler ran a hand through his hair, anxiety mixing with a flicker of excitement. "But what if I mess it up? I've never—"

"Tyler," Tristian interrupted, stepping closer, his tone earnest and soothing. "This isn't about perfection; it's about connection. Trust me. Your voice matters as much as mine in this."

"And what if your mother rejects the request?" Tyler asked.

"She cant..that's why this might be our only chance...and this isn't a fail safe either.." Tristian answers "but they still wont have a choice but to listen."

"Alright.." Tyler said quietly, trusting in the witch he seems to have only just met.

"For now we need to lay low and get a few things... they don't know what we are up to and we only have 6 hours to do it." Tristian said, looking around the dense woods.

Trials and Tribulations

They moved swiftly through the underbrush, the shadows stretching long as the sun began to set, casting an eerie glow over the forest. As they navigated the labyrinth of trees, Tyler's heart pounded in tandem with the urgency of their situation. Each step felt like a countdown, every rustle in the leaves sending prickles of unease rippling down his spine. "What do we need?" he asked, his voice steadying as adrenaline surged.

"We'll need some quartz," Tristian replied, leading Tyler towards a hidden glade he seemed to know intimately. "It helps amplify the spell's potency when charged under the night sky. And some sage—cleansing herbs will strengthen our intention." He paused, his gaze fierce. "We cannot risk any dark energy infiltrating our bond."

Tyler nodded, now resolute. With every moment spent at Tristian's side, he felt a fierce energy building within him, a conviction that reassured him of his place in this chaotic narrative. As the last rays of sunlight dipped below the horizon, they emerged into the glade, a sacred space pulsing with untapped potential. The air crackled with magic, an electric thrill that merged their fate in this desperate hour.

"Here," Tristian said, kneeling to inspect the ground, his fingers brushing over the red pebbles of quartz scattered like stars on earth. "If we do this right, they'll recognize our bond. We just need to be brave enough to show them."

"But what if they still...?" Tyler's voice trailed off, anxiety threading through his resolve. Tristian looked up, his eyes a warm green, steady as a lighthouse.

"Then we'll fight for it." Triaitan replied.

Tristian I hate to have you do this but I need you to turn and find us sage, there should be some near but it's too dark for me to know exactly where.

'"Tristian.. I don't know if I will be able to just turn here.." Tyler said embarrassed.

"Why not? Haven't you ever just gone all wolfy before/" He sighed becoming confused.

"Sure, but not with you watching!" Tyler countered, shifting his weight nervously. "It feels... vulnerable."

"Vulnerable?" Tristian scoffed playfully, a soft grin breaking through the tension. "You're a werewolf! Embrace it! You're strong and magnificent. We can't do this without all the pieces in place."

Tyler sighed, running a hand through his tousled hair. "Okay, okay. Just remember, the last time I shifted, it was..."

"Awesome?" Tristian finished, raising an eyebrow.

"More like terrifying," Tyler replied with a smirk. "But fine, I'll do it." He took a deep breath, the scent of moss and damp earth filling his lungs. "Here goes nothing."

Tristian stepped back, watching intently as the transformation began. "I've got you," he encouraged, his voice a soothing balm against Tyler's doubts.

With a surge of energy, Tyler let the wolf inside him emerge. His bones elongated, muscles shifted, and a rush of raw power coursed through him. As he completed the metamorphosis, he felt an exhilarating rush of freedom.

"Wow," Tristian gasped, eyes wide as he took in the sleek form before him. "You look incredible."

Tyler growled softly, his wolfish instincts taking over, but he focused on Tristian's voice. *I need you to find the sage*

Tyler's grayish white form sniffed in the air,his senses sharpened as he tuned in to the earthy scents surrounding them. The faintest hint of sage wafted through the underbrush, a comforting balm amid the wild energy crackling in his veins. He could feel Tristian's gaze on him, the warmth wrapping around his wolf like an embrace, pushing any remnants of doubt away. With a deep inhale, Tyler pushed off through the foliage, his instincts guiding him deeper into the woods.

The shadows danced around him as he moved, the moon rising to unveil the path ahead. Each step was both exhilarating and primal, the spirit of the wolf singing in his blood. Tyler felt anchored, bound to the earth and sky, a protector in this enchanted night. He darted beneath branches, gaining momentum until he reached a small clearing where wisps of silver-leaved sage grew thickly, while a silvery glow shimmered in the moonlight.

As he wove through the plants, delight surged within him. This was his heritage, the wolf part of him thriving under the cloak of night. He began to gather the sage, carefully plucking the leaves with his teeth rather than claws, reveling in the thrill of simply being. Tyler brought the leaves to Tristian laying them at his feet. "Good pet." Tristian thanked him with an evil smirk. Tristian slowly petted the gray wolf before it slowly turned into Tylers hair. Tyler stayed kneeled at Tristians feet enjoying the attention, enjoying tristian's touch. "Come Tyler, we must dress for the Tribunal." Trisitan said quietly.

"I don't have anything else to wear.." Tyler said in confusion.

"Well that's the great thing about magic isn't it wolf boy." Tristian said with a smile.

With a flick of his wrist, Tristian summoned the shimmering threads of magic that tangled around them. The air shimmered like heat rising from pavement on a summer day, and in moments, the fabric of reality rippled. Tyler blinked, unsure of what to expect. A rush of colors enveloped him, and then, standing before him was not the frayed hoodie he'd worn earlier, but a flowing ensemble woven with the hues of twilight and dawn—a blend of deep blue and soft lavender that wrapped around his form like a second skin. It hugged his body in all the right places, accentuating his newfound confidence that shone through both human and wolf.

Tyler stared, marveling at how perfectly it fit—how it felt to be adorned in something that made him look and feel powerful. "I've never worn anything like this before," he admitted, awe lacing his voice.

"Good. You need to feel magnificent because tonight, we're walking into the Tribunal as equals," Tristian replied, his voice filled with a mix of pride and challenge. He stepped back, taking in the sight of Tyler, and his expression softened. "You've embraced who you are, and that's the strongest magic of all."

Tyler's heart raced. Was it the thrill of the impending confrontation or the undeniable spark between them? Both instincts urged him forward. "Let's do this," he growled softly, every ounce of resolve igniting within him. As they moved closer to the land where the coven would meet, Tyler's senses heightened. The night thrummed with tension, and he could almost taste the apprehension in the air mingled with scents of pine and moss. "What should I say?" he asked nervously.

"Just be yourself," Tristian said, his tone firm yet gentle. "Trust in your strength, and together, we'll challenge them." Tyler nodded, inhaling deeply to steady the storm inside him and feeling the warmth of Tristian's magic fluttering beside him, ready for whatever lay ahead. The two of them stepped forward into the future, ready to confront the trials waiting for them.

***

"I need answers, now!" Marcus bellowed towards his front line of wolves.

"We have reason to believe that the with took him to the witch lands, Sir.." The pack informant said as he tried not to show fear in front of his alpha.

"Why haven't we moved for him yet?" Marcus growled, his eyes narrowing at the informant.

"He's under a powerful spell, Alpha. A binding charm, and the witch's territory is—"

"Dangerous," Marcus interrupted, pacing like a caged lion. "I know. But we can't just stand here and wait for this to unravel. He's my son!"

"I can lead a small unit into their lands, Marcus," one of the pack's warriors, Elena, offered, stepping forward with resolve. "We're trained for combat, and if anyone can break through their defenses, it's us."

"It's too risky, Elena," Marcus snapped, his fury palpable. "What if they capture you? Capture any of us? We can't afford that!"

"You think I don't know risk?" Elena shot back, her tone fierce. "We're wolves! The longer we wait, the more power they have over Tyler. We owe it to him to act!"

Marcus halted, turning to face her fully. "This isn't just about strength or bravery. This is magic we're dealing with. If they discover our approach—"

"Then we'll be swift and fierce," Elena interrupted again, determination radiating from her.

Marcus stroked his chin.

"Fine." Marcus growled as he stepped down from where he was standing.

"I want my son back alive...and unharmed.," Marcus continued getting closer to Elena.

"And if you fail me..I promise it will be a life threatening mistake." Marcus finished, his eyes glowing red staring at the ferocious she- wolf.

"Oh, and take Ethan, he is diverse and all of our treaties and laws. He will make sure you don't fuck it up."

Elena nodded and swiftly turned her back to prepare for the heist.

***

A Witch's Song

The witch and wolf stood together looking at the grand oak door that kept them from the open wood, and the Tribunal. The building was well lit with torches that staggered along the large door.

"Are you ready?" Tristian asked as he looked at Tyler, the determination in his emerald eyes mingling with traces of anxiety.

"Ready as I'll ever be," Tyler replied, his voice steady despite the butterflies in his stomach.

"Remember, we're stronger together," Tristian reminded him, placing a supportive hand on Tyler's arm. "Whatever happens in there, stand tall."

Taking a deep breath, Tyler nodded. "I will. For us."

With their hands intertwined, they approached the great oak door, the weight of their future pressing upon them. Just as Tristian was about to push it open, Tyler hesitated. "What if they reject us?"

Tristian's grip tightened. "We will face it together, no matter the outcome," he affirmed, his voice low but full of resolve. "Sometimes love is the fiercest rebellion."

Tyler offered a small smile, comforted by Tristian's unwavering belief. "Let's show them what we can do."

With a shared nod, they pushed the door wide open. The room inside was cavernous and filled with witches seated in a semicircle, their expressions a mix of curiosity and skepticism. The air buzzed with magical energy, thickening with every second they stood there.

Thirteen faces, some wrinkled and some looking filled with youth, Tristians mother at the center of the table. Tyler gulped as his wolf whimpered.

The atmosphere was electric as Tyler and Tristian stepped into the dimly lit chamber, each of the witches fixing their gaze upon the intruders. A palpable hush fell over the room, broken only by the soft flicker of flames from the torches lining the walls. Tyler's heart raced with uncertainty; these were the very beings who had cast him into turmoil with their binding spells, yet beneath their scrutinizing stares, he sensed a flicker of intrigue—a glimmer of hesitance.

"We've come to speak before the Tribunal," Tristian stated, his voice strong, yet shaking slightly under the weight of the moment. "I stand in support of Tyler, the son of the alpha wolf, and we seek to break the bonds that hold him captive." His words echoed, filling the space with courage woven through vulnerability.

The eldest witch, her silver hair cascading over her shoulders, leaned forward, her piercing gaze locking onto Tritian. "You dare to approach us, with that...wolf?" she questioned, voice sharp as the edge of a blade. "What makes you think your love can stand against the magic of our coven?" she asked, looking now at Tyler.

Tyler inhaled deeply, the scent of herbs and lingering enchantment filling his lungs. "Because love is magic in its truest form," he asserted, feeling the weight of both fear and hope surge within him. "And together, we can create a new world—not built on ancient grudges, but on acceptance. I refuse to let fear dictate my life any longer." The words spilled forth, each syllable an incantation of strength he never knew he possessed.

Tristian's grip tightened around his hand, grounding him. The witches murmured to one another, their voices a whirlpool of skepticism and surprise. Tyler could feel the tides turning as the energy shifted, both frightening and exhilarating, and through it all, he hung onto Tristian's magic like a lifeline.

"And what say you Tristian. Why should we allow you to be together as an interspecies couple which threatens us all." Another witch asked, one with youth in her features.

Tristian straightened his shoulders, meeting the challenging gaze of the young witch with determination. "Because we are stronger together than we ever could be apart," he responded, his voice ringing with confidence. "This isn't just about us; it's about rewriting the narrative of our worlds. Love knows no boundaries, and it's time for the coven to embrace that."

The eldest witch arched an eyebrow, pondering his words. "You speak of love as if it's a shield, but it can also be a weapon. How can you assure us you won't become a danger to our kind?"

Tyler's heart pounded. "We're not here to harm anyone. I know what it feels like to be shunned for who I am—being a wolf and feeling trapped. I refuse to let that fear control my life anymore. We want to create a bridge, to foster understanding." He took a step closer to the semicircle of witches, channeling his wolf's strength. "If you give us a chance, we can prove it. I can't let my father's expectations dictate who I am."

"Expectations can be hard to cast aside," the young witch replied. "What guarantee do we have that you won't turn on us?"

"None," Tristian interjected passionately. "But that's the beauty of trust. It's a leap into the unknown." He let the silence settle for a moment.

*****

The wolves stood at the wood lining that led to the tribunal house.

Elena halted the line as she looked around her surroundings.

"Are we sure this is a good idea Elena?" Ethan, the pack informant asked.

Elena turned, her eyes fierce yet filled with uncertainty. "There's no choice, Ethan. If we don't act now, we could lose Tyler forever."

Ethan raised an eyebrow, skepticism written all over his face. "But charging in without a plan? That's reckless!"

"Reckless?" Elena scoffed, crossing her arms. "Is waiting for the witches to decide Tyler's fate also a genius plan?"

"Are we even sure about the witches' intentions? What if they don't have him?" Ethan pressed, his voice rising. "We shouldn't jump to conclusions."

"Not jump," Elena insisted, shaking her head. "We have to dive headfirst. We can't just stand around and hope for a miracle!"

Ethan leaned closer, lowering his voice. "But if you fail... If it's a trap—"

"Then I'll die fighting for him," Elena shot back, her determined stare piercing. "We're wolves! If we can't protect our own, then what are we?"

Ethan sighed, running a hand through his hair, frustration evident. "Fine. But you know it's not just about strength. We need strategy."

"Strategy? We have no time for games!" Elena huffed, pacing back and forth. "Tyler is strong, but he's alone among them. He needs us now more than ever."

Ethan placed a hand on her shoulder, his expression softening.

Elena gave him a stern look causing Ethan to slowly remove his hand.

Elena turned around facing the whole pack. "This pack will follow the orders of the alpha, even if that means death. If any of you coware, you will meet a death sentence before you can even stand trial for your treason." She finished, her voice stern and with an objective.

****

"Witches, wolves, and even vampires have all lived apart for over a century now. What makes you two young men think you should be given special treatment?" Another of the thirteen spoke, this one wrinkled with magically red hair.

"Because our love is a force you've underestimated," Tristian replied, fire igniting in his emerald eyes. "We're not seeking special treatment; we're asking for a chance—a chance to prove that unity can be stronger than the ancient grudges."

The eldest witch leaned back, eyes narrowed but contemplative. "And if you fail?"

Tyler straightened, his voice steady, despite the tremor of his heart. "Then you can hold us accountable. But I promise we will fight for our place, to show you that our worlds can coexist without fear."

A murmur rippled through the audience of witches, some exchanging glances of intrigue. The younger witch piped up, "What if your love falls apart? What then?"

Tristian stepped forward, chin held high. "Love is never perfect, but it's forged in trials. We'll face those trials together. Isn't that what life's about?"

"A noble sentiment, but romantic ideals won't safeguard you from the reality of magic," the eldest witch warned, her expression hardening. "Magic is unpredictable, often dark."

"There's darkness in every heart, which we can choose to illuminate," Tyler interjected, passion fuelling his words. "I've felt lost, alone, and misunderstood in my own world. If we can embrace our differences rather than let them tear us apart, we could become something greater."

"Enlightening words, yet they belong to a child untested in real adversity."

"Yes but.." Tyler started before a gavel came down.

"Silence, we have talked enough." Tristian's mother Celeste finally spoke.

"We will deliberate and then give you a decision." She spoke as the witches all turned towards the center and sat in silence.

Tyler looked around confused as he waited for their words of discussion.

"Tylers what's.." Tyler started.

"Witches can communicate telepathically, very much like wolf packs." Tristian answered as he rubbed his hands together not knowing what the Thirteen were saying.

Tyler's heart raced in anticipation, every beat echoing the rising tension in the chamber. The air felt dense with uncertainty, as if the very essence of magic hung between them, waiting to be released or contained. He stole a glance at Tristian, whose brow furrowed in deep concentration, the flicker of his candlelit aura casting shadows on his face. Tyler reached out, fingers grazing Tristian's, igniting a warmth that briefly calmed his racing mind. He was here, standing beside the one person who believed in the possibility of a world united, and for a moment, that was enough to buoy his spirits.

The silent chatter amongst the witches faded into a heavy silence, the only sound punctuating the atmosphere being the minor crackling of Tristian's spells dancing in the corners of the room. Suddenly, Celeste lifted her gaze, piercing green eyes locking onto Tyler, a weighty pause preceding her words. "Your fervor is commendable, but it lacks the weight of experience. How can we crown such naivete with hope?"

Tyler clenched his fists, courage overpowering the doubt threatening to swallow him whole. "Experience is learned through action, through the pain of our pasts. I may be young, but I won't stand by while hatred breeds more hatred. If Tristian and I can show you the strength of our bond, maybe—just maybe—it can spark a change in this world where nothing else has."

The murmurs resumed, some witches leaning in while others frowned. Tristian squeezed Tyler's hand firmly, as if offering him strength. "Let us be a living testament," he urged, eyes shimmering with determination. "Give us the chance to show you that togetherness can conquer even the deepest divisions."

The powerful witch considered their words, a flicker of realization crossing her features. "A gamble, this love of yours," she intoned, scanning the faces of The Thirteen.

"I'm sorry this request has been denied." His mothers voice said as she brought the gavel down.

As the gavel dropped, the old wooden doors opened as a pile of wolves filed in.

Elena put up her first holding the pack in a line.

"Well good, then we were just in time. Celeste we are here to reclaim, whom your son thought was his for the taking." She said softly but with an evil smirk.

Tyler's heart sank at the sight of Elena and the pack flooding into the chamber, each wolf's presence a reminder of the anxiety clawing at him.

"What are you doing!" Tristian's voice trembled with dismay.

Elena stepped forward, eyes gleaming with a mix of mischief and intent, a confident smirk dancing on her lips. "We're here to bring our dear Tyler back. I didn't think you'd be foolish enough to try and take him from us."

"Foolish?" Tyler stepped forward, anger igniting within him. "You have no idea what we're trying to accomplish here!"

"Oh, I think I do," Elena replied, her tone dripping with condescension. "Playing house with the witches? How charming. You think they'll accept you? They're just using you to further their own ends."

"You're wrong!" Tristian snapped, stepping protectively in front of Tyler. "We're fighting for a future free from war—"

"A future that starts with you being a threat to us! You don't belong here, Tyler," Elena shot back, stepping towards Tyler, a growl escaping her lips.

"I belong wherever I choose!" Tyler exclaimed, feeling his wolf surge to the surface, the duality of his existence igniting a fire in his chest. "I've struggled long enough to be accepted!"

The rows of witches murmured, their expressions caught between intrigue and war.

"Tristian do something.." Tyler begged, his eyes betraying him as they started to water.

Tristian looked at the witches before clearing his throat and speaking loudly to all thirteen witches. "I'm claiming my right to sing Song of the Souls." he finished gulping loudly.

The witches almost gasped as they whispered between each other.

A hush fell over the chamber as an array of intrigued expressions swept across the faces of the witches.

"What do you mean?" the elderly witch, Celeste, questioned, her voice steady yet intrigued. "The Song of the Souls is a powerful incantation. Are you certain you understand its implications, Tristian?"

Tristian met her gaze, his determination unwavering. "I do. And I'm willing to sing it to prove the depth of our bond. If the magic of our love can resonate through our souls, it could unite us."

The witches looked at eachother. Gwen, the witch to the right of Celeste looked at her. "I don't think we have a choice, there's never been a rule that it couldn't be done between species..no one ever thought it would happen." she said.

Celeste sighed and nodded. "Very well."

"I think this has gone on long enough.." Elena said as she looked towards two of the stronger wolves. They started approaching Tyler as Ethan started.

"Elena I don't think we should.." Ethan said, reaching for the three of them.

Before they could fully approach the witch's eyes all glowed and sent a force field sending the three wolves back and building a wall of energy.

"We aren't allowed to interrupt an ongoing tribunal.." Ethan finished as they all stared at the wall of energy.

Elena growled before nodding as she crossed her arms.

"Are you sure you're ready?" Celeste asked one last time to the boys. Tristian nodded.

"Very well... get in place." She finished.

Tristian smiled and led Tyler to the direct center of the floor. "Sit across from me." he whispered.

Together they sat in the middle of the floor. Tristian lit their sage and let the smoke rise. He then laid a bowl in the center and put their quartz in.

Tristian nodded to his mother, in return his mother nodded to the other witchs.

A deep note came suddenly from the witch the furthest the left. Next to her a note only slightly higher, the next witch a higher. These notes went down the line till the last which was singing an octave just below disappearing from human range. Magic soon started flowing through the air as The Thirteen met an array of notes.

Tristian looked at Tyler. "Just follow my lead...the song lies in your heart."

Tritian started in a low bartone, his voice making a song with all the other witches notes, it almost seems to say "Please." As Tritians notes rang, the crystals in the bowl started shaking as an invisible wind began to blow. Tritian continued singing before looking at Tyler and nodding.

Tyler sighed before reaching down and starting his notes. Tyler let out a higher note than Trisitians, one that started to harmonize with Tritians causing the bowl of crystals to glow brighter. Tendrils of energies started expanding from the crystals. The walls of the building shook as the matching harmonies of witches and wolves swarmed the building. The tendrils of energy started taking forms, twisting and swirling around each other. As the witches sang and the young men harmonized the crystals and tendrils of energy grew brighter and brighter until at last the energy exploded into the room ,forming the image of a tree. The tree crackled for a moment before exploding and scattering above their heads to form the patterns of the Aurora Borealis. The witches stopped singing, as did Tyler and Tristian as everyone just looked up at the dancing lights in amazement.

Elena blinked, her skepticism momentarily forgotten as she looked up, mesmerized by the shimmering lights. "What... is this?" she breathed, astonished.

"It's magic," Tyler replied, awash in wonder. "Our magic."

Tristian turned back to the group, the intensity in his eyes now softened with hope. "This is proof that our love can resonate beyond all boundaries. Look, the auroras... they symbolize unity."

A murmuring began among the witches, their expressions shifting from doubt to contemplation. The young witch from before stepped forward, her brow furrowed. "Is this... really possible? A connection like this?"

Tyler found his voice, emboldened by the shimmering aurora. "Yes! We can bridge the divide between our worlds. Just look at what we created together—it's beautiful because it's a mix of our powers."

Elena crossed her arms, skepticism creeping back in. "But what if this is temporary? What if the feelings don't last?"

"They can last," Tristian insisted. "Love takes effort, commitment, but it's worth fighting for. We're willing to show you that." His eyes flicked to Tyler, who nodded in agreement.

Celeste, still observing with an appraising gaze, broke the silence. "The spectacle is undeniably powerful. Yet it doesn't erase history. There's pain in these divides and I'm sorry but we will not let this happen." she said looking down at the boys. "You were given the right to perform the song, that does not mean we must accept its outcome. Tyler will be leaving with his pack tonight."." She finished as she looked at the two young men and then at Elena.

Soon the barrier, holding the wolves back, dropped and they started in on Tyler to take him back to the pack house.

"Stop!" Tristian yelled, a boom that shook the room with magical intensity.

"Fine then mother you leave me no choice." He said starring Celeste deep in the eyes. "We request to find the stone of Ohara." he said as he gritted his teeth. The witches gasp, as did the wolf informant Ethan.

"You can't be serious Tristian, that journey could kill you both." His mother started as the murmurs between the witches council erupted quietly.

"What's the Stone of Ohara?" Elena asked openly to anyone who would listen.

"It is a rare moonstone, said to be able to mend anything broken, even the disparities between witches and wolves. It was said to be the most powerful tool to the one who used it. It is said to answer both witches...and wolves." Celeste spoke, her voice calm yet almost shaking.

"I'm sorry but that sounds like a fairy tale, and we have to get Tyler back." Elena said, stepping forward.

"Actually, we can't," Ethan spoke.

"The moonstone is said to be very real, and when the war between witches, wolves, and vampires started, it was written that anyone who seeks the moon stone to bring peace must be allowed to try." Ethan finished as he scratched his head.

Tristian met Elena's gaze with unyielding determination. "This isn't just a fairy tale to us; it's our only hope," he insisted, his voice steady despite the tensions swirling around them. "If the stone truly can mend the rift between our peoples, then we have to try. If it means risking our lives for a chance at unity, then it's worth it." Tyler felt a surge of pride for the witch at his side. He admired Tristian's courage, even as uncertainty gnawed at his own heart.

"Where can we find it?" Tyler asked, his pulse quickening with anticipation. The thought of venturing out into the unknown, seeking a legendary stone that could alter their destinies, seemed both thrilling and terrifying. He glanced at Celeste, a mixture of doubt and respect in her eyes.

Celeste took a deep breath, wrestling with the responsibility of her position. "The legends speak of it being hidden in the ancient forest, deep within the heart of the Elderwood Grove. But beware—many dangers lurk in the shadows, and the trials you face may challenge more than just your strength." Her warning hung over them like a dark cloud, yet there was an undeniable glimmer of hope igniting within Tyler.

"Then we'll go tonight," Tristian declared, resolute, challenging the witches to argue. "We'll navigate through those dangers together, us against the odds. If we make it, not only will we bring back the stone, but we'll show everyone that we can be stronger and united." The group fell silent, the air thick with a mix of apprehension and anticipation. Tyler reached for Tristian's hand, their fingers intertwining as they prepared to take the leap into uncertainty. Together, they could forge a new path, defying fate and turning myths into reality.

The Journey Begins

As they stood there, hand in hand, the whispers of the council faded into a heavy silence. Tyler felt the weight of every gaze upon him, pressing down like a thick fog. He could sense the unease rippling through the room, but his heart thudded with a wild rhythm of potential. "What if we fail?" he thought, the question curling around his subconscious like a serpent, tightening ever so slightly. But Tristian's warm grip seemed to dissolve the doubt, feeding a flicker of confidence within him.

Celeste, still processing the shift of power in the room, began to speak again, her voice softening. "If you choose to embark on this journey, know that you risk more than just your lives; you risk everything you understand about your identities." The subtle authority in her tone was tempered by a flicker of understanding. "But perhaps, in the midst of this chaos, there lies a path for reconciliation."

Eager murmurs began to rise among the witches, some fueled by ambition, others by fear. Tyler caught snippets of their conversations—talk of dusty tomes and ancient magic. Then, Ethan stepped forward, his brow furrowed. "I can't let you go unprepared. Even if you believe you can face the challenges ahead, we owe it to you to ensure you are equipped." His eyes searched both their faces. "Know this: the Elderwood Grove does not suffer trespassers lightly."

With that, the dynamic shifted. The witches convened in quick huddles, gathering supplies and vital artifacts. Tyler watched Tristian as he cleared a path for them, his chin tilted defiantly. With a final squeeze of Tyler's hand, Tristian turned to the witches, his eyes sparkling with determination. "We're going to show them that unity isn't just possible, it's necessary."

As they finally set their eyes on the doorway leading to the night air, Tyler felt a swell of hope. The road ahead promised more than peril; it glittered with the possibility of change, molded by the strength of newfound love. Together, they stepped out, embracing the darkness that awaited them, each heartbeat echoing a promise to bridge the divides that had kept them apart for far too long.

The boys took the supplies and placed them in an enchanted bag."Your father will not let this go easily Tyler." Elena said as her eyes stared into Tyler's soul."

"Good thing this isn't about him." Tyler replied as he passed her towards the door and into the unknown with his silvered hair witch.

Tristan reached for the handle before Celeste appeared next to him. "Please be careful, you will not be the thing that has access to magic out there." She whispered before grabbing his shoulder lightly. "I love you my son." she finished before moving her soft hand to his cheek, brushing it slightly.

Tyler felt a warmth spread through him at Tristians mother's words, a flicker of reassurance amidst the uncertainty. He turned to Tristian, whose face reflected a mix of determination and concern."Are you ready for this?" Tyler asked, locking eyes with him."More than ever," Tristian replied, his voice steady. "Together, we can handle whatever comes our way."

Elena stepped closer, her expression shifting from skepticism to reluctant admiration. "Just... be careful. You don't know what's out there.""Are you worried about us, Elena?" Tyler quipped, a small smile creeping onto his lips."Don't push your luck, wolf," she shot back, though her voice held a hint of camaraderie. "Just remember, the further you go from the pack, the less safe you'll be."Tristian chuckled softly at their banter. "We'll be fine. We have each other, and that's what matters.""Focus on your mission, you two," Celeste cautioned, the underlying concern in her gaze tangible. "The Elderwood Grove holds challenges beyond your imagination. Trust your instincts... and one another."

With a deep breath, Tristian nodded. "We will. We won't give in to fear. We have a bond that's stronger than any trial we'll face.""Then go already!" Elena urged, stepping aside as the door creaked open. "The longer you wait, the more peril we will be because of your father." she said before rolling her eyes."Lets go..pet" Tristian said smiling at TylerTyler nodded and together they stepped out the Oak doors and towards their quest.****"He WHAT?" Marcus yelled causing all of the other wolves to shake and bow their heads, not willing to make eye contact."Well Sir we didn't.." Ethan tried to chime in before the alpha's claws shot through his hands and came across Ethan's face leaving a very noticeable scratch that started bleeding immediately.

"Would anyone else like to try and justify this?" he asked sternly as Ethan now lied on the floor, holding his face, whimpering."My Alpha.. we truly had no choice." Elena started as she bowed in front of him.Marcus growled and raised his hand before sighing."This was your job Elena...be glad that I'm sparing my hand to you at this moment. He has three days to be back. If my son is not back in that time Elena, you better hope that leaving you scarred is all I do." he said looking down at her."Yes Sir." she replied."Now, get up and take Ethan to medical.." he finished before sitting down at his desk.Elena nodded and went to Ethan as everyone else started to leave the room.***"Should we be doing this?" Tyler asked as the boys walked side by side into the dark woods."What do you mean pet?" Tristian asked." Well, why cant we just run away?""My mom is one of the most powerful coven leaders in the Country...and your father will never give you freedom willingly." Tristian replied, his tone clipped.Tyler nodded."Why must you insist on calling me pet.? Tyler asked as he tried to keep up with witch .Tristian paused, a playful smirk dancing on his lips. "Because you're my little werewolf companion on this grand adventure. Besides, it suits you," he teased, winking."Is that so?" Tyler replied, pretending to be offended, though a smile tugged at the corners of his mouth. "Last I checked, I'm not a pet. I'm a werewolf, destined for greatness—or doom.""Oh, come on. You know you love it," Tristian laughed, his voice echoing softly among the ancient trees. "And who wouldn't want to be a 'pet' to a powerful witch?"Tyler sighed dramatically, brightening his smile. "Guess it's better than being called a traitor, which is what I'll be if this doesn't work.""We'll make it work," Tristian reassured him, squeezing his hand. "Together, we're unstoppable. We just need to believe in our bond, no matter what darkness lurks ahead.""Right," Tyler muttered, trying to muster confidence. "But this journey feels like leaping into the abyss without a tether. I'm not like you, Tristian. I have so much to unravel about myself.""That's exactly why we're in this together," Tristian replied earnestly. "You're not just a wolf; you're bold and brave. Trust in that strength. And don't forget—I'm here with you.""So how was the Stone originally lost in the first place?" Tyler asked as they continued down the dark path.Tristian frowned, the flickering shadows of the trees dancing behind him. "The stories say it was hidden to protect it from those who would misuse its powers," he explained, his voice serious. "During the war, chaos reigned. The stone was lost in the turmoil, and with it, a chance at peace."Tyler shivered, a chill running down his spine. "So we're hunting for something that could be anywhere... and might not even exist?""Yes, but think about it, Tyler. If it does exist, we have a chance to change everything," Tristian said, his determination shining through. "No one thought we could create the auroras, yet we did."Tyler nodded, absorbing Tristian's words. "I guess you're right. If we can harness our powers together, maybe we can find the stone too."Tristian turned to Tyler, his eyes gleaming with encouragement. "Exactly. And remember, it's not just about the stone. It's about redefining what our worlds mean. We're proving that love can conquer any divide.""Wouldn't it be easier if our families just got along? Why do we have to do this?" Tyler asked, a hint of frustration bubbling."Because they've built these walls long before we came along," Tristian replied, his gaze steady on the path ahead. "Destroying those barriers takes time, courage, and unity."Tristian walked with Tyler scared to think about a descion he might have to make if they found the Stone, to truly unite the species...or take the power for himself. Could he ever truly betray the boy who was actually growing on Tristian. Could they ever truly be more? Tristian shook the thought as the bushed rustled behind them.Tyler's heart raced as the underbrush snapped ominously, sending a wave of anxiety coursing through him. "Did you hear that?" He stopped in his tracks, his ears straining for another sound among the whispers of the wind. The forest felt alive, but not in the comforting way he had hoped.Tristian halted beside him, the smirk evaporating from his face. "Stay close," he whispered, the playful tone now replaced with a steely resolve. "Whatever it is, we can handle it. Together."Just as Tyler inhaled to steady himself, three shadowy figures emerged from the tangled roots and ferns, their eyes glinting like embers in the night's darkness. Tyler's instincts kicked in, a primal urge to shift battling with the very human need for safety. "What do we do? Are they part of your coven?" he hissed, adrenaline flooding his words.A low, guttural laugh echoed through the trees, and the figures stepped into the faint moonlight, revealing a trio of malevolent witches, their eyes narrowed with disdain. "Looks like the lovebirds think they can run away to find a powerful artifact," one of them sneered, a twisted grin curling on his lips. "But you're in way over your heads, little boy and his pet."Tristian took a step in front of Tyler, his body tense, ready to protect. "I won't let you intimidate us," he replied, his voice steady but edged with anger. "We're not afraid of you."As the air crackled with tension, Tyler found strength in Tristian's unwavering stance beside him. The thought of the Stone faded for a moment, replaced by the re-alization that they were stronger together, facing whatever darkness dared to confront them. "We'll show you the power of love over hatred," Tyler declared, his wolf instincts rising to the surface.With a burst of courage, the duo squared their shoulders, ready to face the gathering storm."Ah the Ember sisters.." Tristian started as he started at them. "Not sure if you are aware but you aren't allowed to interfear with this quest.""Oh we know," the taller of the sisters spoke, her hair as red as fire."But if you were to go missing, who would even know." She finished.The moment hung in the air, thick with hostility. Tyler could feel his heart pounding in his chest, a rhythm that matched the sounds of the forest—the rustling leaves, the distant howls of wolves, and the impending clash of magic. "What do you want?" Tyler challenged, his voice stronger than he felt."We want what you're after," the red-haired sister replied, stepping forward, her presence menacing as shadow cloaked her form. "The Stone's power belongs to our coven. It can reshape destinies, turn tides of war. Why waste it on a love story?"Tristian's jaw clenched, but he stood resolute. "Because love is stronger than any stone, and it can rewrite the narrative you think you control."The Ember sister laughed, the sound sharp and mocking. "So naive, boy. You think your precious bond can shield you? I can crush your heart before it ever beats again."As she raised her hand, a spark ignited in the air, swirling like a tornado of embers. Tyler gritted his teeth, feeling the hunt within him awaken, but more than that, he felt a connection with Tristian—a pulse of energy that surged between their fingertips. He glanced at Tristian, who held his gaze with fierce determination, and it was then Tyler realized that this wasn't just about survival. This was about choosing the light they both craved against the dark."Together," Tyler said fiercely, his voice a whisper woven with resolve, as the air thickened with magic. He felt the intoxicating urge to shift, to unleash the wolf within him, but he held it steady, channeling it instead into the space they shared. "Let's show them what we're made of."With a shared nod, they stood shoulder to shoulder, breathing in the moment before a storm, embracing their power, and igniting a spark of change that could light up their worlds. The elements around them buzzed with anticipation, ready to follow their lead."Unfortunely, we cant let you do that" One of the sisters spoke as her hand swirled catching the night with it. "Now sit, pet." she replied bringing her hand down forcing Tyler to the ground."Pity...Wolves really don't need concern them self with witches." the last sister spoke with a laughter to her voice. Tristian felt his blood boil before stepping forward, the wind howling around them."If anyone gets to control him, it will be me!" Tristian spat before electricity sparked at his finger tips. "Daemones produent. Figura, forma et capto" He muttered, and as he did the ground filled with fog. From the fog dark shapes started emerging grabbing the sisters by their throats. Tristians eyes blazed a fiery blue. "If it were just me we could have a real battle, not when you bring Tyler into it." Tyler got up as he stared at the scene. The sisters were choking as more figures formed grabbing their entire bodies. He glanced at Tristian who was watching this scene with glee. " Accipere, Tenere, Mergi." He said to the shadows. The shadow grasped the witches and covered their mouths as they started dragging the sisters down into the fog. It wasn't long before their forms disappeared completely.The fog faded, their bodies nowhere to be found before Tristian collapsed onto his knees breathing hard from the energy spent.Tyler ran to his side."Tristian..what happened to them." He asked, never having seen that kind of magic."Don't worry they wont bother us anymore." he replied, voice clipped and stern.Tyler twisted his thumbs before starring down at him. "That was scary.""Well they tried to hurt you." Tristian replied before looking up at Tylers soft face."Come here.. I need energy." Tristian said softly trying to get to his feet."I don't know...what you just did was..""Now!" He yelled towards Tyler, his eyes still glowing.Tyler walked over to Trisitan and got down to his level."Good boy." Tristian replied before looking at Tyler and grabbing him and pulling him into a kiss. Their bond came alive as Tyler moaned gently into the witch's mouth. Tristian kissed the wolf hard before starting to suck Tyler's energy force. The energy flowed from Tyler into Tristian as they both kissed each other passionately. Tyler grabbed at Tristian silver hair needing more, his wolf needing more. "Enough." Tristian said sternly as he pulled their kiss apart. "If we keep doing that you will be too weak to walk." Tristian finished as he stood to his feet.'Wha.." Tyler started, standing up and losing balance."It's an energy transference spell. You will be fine in a minute." Tristian said, helping Tyler to his feet. "But thanks for the kiss... pet." Tristian said, smiling at Tyler. Tyler's feelings shot through him like the reverberations of a drum, leaving him exhilarated yet disoriented. The remnants of the fog dissipated into the air, and he felt the cool night wrapping around them like an embrace, a sharp contrast to the heat that lingered between them. He leaned against Tristian, gratitude swelling within him. "You really saved us back there," he whispered, mingling with confusion as he tried to process what had just happened. Tristian offered a playful smirk, which offered Tyler a sense of reassurance even amidst the chaos. "I can handle myself, but I'm glad you're here," he replied, brushing a hand across Tyler's cheek, grounding him with the warmth of his touch. "We make a good team. But we can't be too reckless; those sisters aren't gone forever, only silenced for now."As the weight of their victory settled within them, Tyler pushed away the remnants of fear swirling inside. "What do we do next?" he asked, his voice steadier now. He could feel the undeniable tugging of fate, the choices they had to make pressing upon them. With Tristian by his side, he realized he didn't have to fight alone.Tristian's expression turned serious, his fiery blue eyes unyielding. "We gather the stone before they return. But first, we need to harness your wolf's strength—trust me, there's more to this energy sharing than mere survival. You're more than just the alpha's son, Tyler; you have a legacy no one else understands." He stepped back, gesturing toward the darkened paths of the forest ahead. "Let's find that path together."With newfound resolve, Tyler nodded, heart racing not just from the fear of what lay ahead, but from the thrilling possibilities of the journey that was unraveling between them—one of magic, danger, and perhaps, even love

Shadows of the Soul

Their walk through the forest was dark and filled with sounds that made the wolf shake at every turn. Trisitan walked in front of Tyler with determination, looking around for any signs of trouble. Tyler caught up to Trisitan and grabbed his arm.

"So, tell me more about this Stone." Tyler said, looking up towards Tristian as he followed.

"It is one of the most powerful magical objects to have existed, it is said to have been made from a piece of all the creatures that made it. Wolves, vampires, and of course witches. It is said that whoever finds the stone would be able to control anything, or anyone they wanted, even groups of people, hence the peace for all."

"So, why hasn't anyone been able to find it?" Tyler asked. Trisitan stopped, focusing his attention on Tyler so that he could explain better.

"It is said that usually the grove gets to everyone before they can get to it." His tone turned grim. There are many different creatures out here, some more powerful than others. Even the Earth itself changes to meet the needs of the stone and hides it." Tristian answered before sighing.

"Why would the Earth hide something that could bring peace?" Tyler asked innocently, his eyes wide.

Tristian pondered for a moment, his gaze distant. "Because peace is often a disguise for control. The Earth knows that power can corrupt, and when one being possesses too much, it can lead to chaos rather than harmony."

Tyler frowned, his brow furrowing in thought. "So, you're saying the stone could bring peace, but it also has the potential to destroy everything?"

"Exactly," Tristian replied, a hint of concern creeping into his voice. "That's why we have to be careful. If we do find it and if it exists, it must be used for the right reasons."

Tyler shivered, feeling the weight of the decision they were pursuing. "And what if we can't handle it? What if it changes us?"

Tristian turned, resting a hand on Tyler's shoulder, his touch warm and reassuring. "That's why we have each other. You remind me of who I am and why I fight. We're already stronger together. We won't let it control us; we'll use it to forge a new destiny."

"Do you really believe that?" Tyler asked, searching Tristian's eyes for reassurance.

"I have to believe it," Tristian said earnestly. "If I don't, then we might as well turn back now."

Tyler inhaled deeply, steadying himself in the face of uncertainty. "Then let's keep going. Together."

For a brief second they locked before Trisitan leaned down and kissed Tyler, their breaths and energies mingling.

"Good pet, now let's keep going, we have a lot of ground to cover."

Tyler nodded and they continued into the dark forest.

As they ventured further into the forest the air only got thicker, the night darker.

"Tristian, I'm scared." Tyler said shyly, making Tristian pause.

"Don't be scared of my pet, I will protect us." Tristian answered as he locked his hand into Tylers.

"I'm not sure something just doesn't feel right.." Tyler responded.

Before Tristian could assure him Tyler heard a laugher, it was small yet low.

"Did you hear that?" Tyler asked as they both looked around. Tristian simply nodded as he looked for the source of the sound.

A rustling in the underbrush caught their attention, and the laughter grew louder—a chilling sound that echoed through the trees, making the hairs on Tyler's neck stand on end. Shadows danced between the branches, twisting in the flickering moonlight, as if teasing them, trying to lure them deeper into the forest's embrace.

"Stay close," Tristian whispered, his voice a mere thread of calm woven into the thick tension hanging between them. He pulled Tyler closer, his arm protectively wrapped around the younger werewolf's shoulders. Together, they advanced cautiously, their breaths mingling with the cool night air.

"Who's there?" Tristian called out, trying to sound confident, but the tremor in his voice betrayed his unease. The laughter stopped abruptly, plunging the forest into suffocating silence. In that moment, the darkness felt alive, as if the very trees had ears and eyes, watching them with malicious intent.

"Perhaps it's a trick of the grove," Tristian continued, his voice low. "We're intruders in this place, and it's known to play host to many dark secrets."

Just as he finished speaking, a dark figure emerged from the shadows, its form twisted and gnarled, eyes gleaming like emeralds in the night.

"Ah, sweet little witch and wolf, wandered too far from home, haven't you?" The figure cackled, the laughter once again echoing ominously through the air. Tyler's heart raced as he instinctively shifted closer to Tristian, his instincts screaming alarm, while Tristian squared his shoulders, ready to confront whatever fate awaited them.

"Who are you?" Tyler demanded, his voice shaky but defiant. The figure leaned closer, revealing a crooked grin that spoke of ancient malice and adoration for chaos.

"I go by many names, but you may call me Saltise." the figure said, stepping out from the brush. It was a tall figure, beautiful with pale alabaster skin. Its eye glowed a deep purple and his back held a pair white wings that folded perfectly together like an angel..

" I am keeper of the fae in this land and I'm afraid I can not let you pass."

Tristian narrowed his eyes, determination etched into his face. "We seek the stone which means.."

"We fae do not follow the laws of the witches or any other creature for that matter. We have been left, our sacred spaces destroyed by those who look more human, when these are our lands. The Earth has chosen not to reveal itself to the like of anyone and we will respect its wishes,unlike you..witch." Saltise spat out.

"Look, we don't want any trouble," Tyler said, trying to keep his voice steady. "We just need to find the stone."

Saltise's laughter rang out again, high-pitched and mocking. "Trouble? Oh, sweet wolf, trouble is all I see here. Do you really think you can waltz into my realm and demand anything? The Earth has its guardians, and you trespass with no regard."

Tristian stepped forward, anger simmering beneath his calm facade. "We'll do what we must. We are not your enemies. We merely seek something that could bring peace."

"Peace, you say?" Saltise raised an eyebrow, skepticism dripping from his words. "That's a delicate word, is it not? So often spoken in the same breath as control. What assurance do you have that you won't become the very tyrants you seek to prevent?"

Tyler swallowed hard, uncertainty creeping in again. "We don't want to control anyone. We just want to protect those we care about."

"Ah, noble sentiments, but do they hold weight in reality?" Saltise replied, the corners of his mouth twitching with malice. "What if I told you that you're as much a puppet in this game as the rest of us? You cannot trust your own desires."

"Stop!" Tristian interjected, his voice sharp with authority. "You may be a keeper, but we have our purpose."

"I'm sorry but unfortunately that purpose isn't good enough." With that he raised his now clawed hand and a swirl of energy engulfed the boys, Tristian struggled against it trying to summon any energy that he left to create a barrier.

"Pathetic, you are no match for me witch.Your kind may only exist by our graciousness" he said before slamming them on the ground with pure energy.

"Please, I will do anything to find the stone." Tristian begged as he looked towards the creature.

"Anything?" Saltise asked, looking between the boys.

Tristian merely nodded as he looked towards Tyler with fear in his eyes.

The creature stared at them for a moment then went back to Tristian.

"I'll make you a deal than boy... I will let you pass into the grove and closer to the stone, but you must leave the wolf with me." Saltise said, his sharp smile turning upwards.

Tyler's heart raced as he looked between the witch and the creature who was trying to make a fearful deal. "You can't do that." he barked at Stalis.

"Shut it!" the creature barked before looking back over to Tristian.

"Tyler.. don't" Tristian started, trying to protect him. "I can't just give him to you.." he remarked back towards Stalis.

"I don't really think that you are in the right position to bargain. Now are you, witch?" he asked as his words twisted with sin.

"Why would you even want me?" Tyler asked, almost as if trying to persuade him a different way.

"I want what every creature wants," Stalis started. "I want control. I can feel the wolf's energy inside of you, even better since you are bonded to a witch.." Stalis finished as he looked towards Tyler with a hunger in his eyes.

"I won't let you have him! I need him, we need to be together to get the stone." Tristian said, trying to crawl towards the fairy.

Instantly Tristian was slammed back to the ground with a powerful force of magic. "You make me bored, now say yes to my deal and I will leave you on your way to get the stone. However, if not then I'm afraid I will just have to kill both of you. I'm making you the deal of a lifetime witch." He said, his voice softening as if he were trying to be kind.

Tristian looked at Stalis and then to Tyler before mouthing the words "Forgive me"

With a glance at the ground Tristian spoke. "You can have him if you let me pass..."

"Tristian, no!" Tyler shouted, his voice trembling as his heart dropped.

"Silence!" Saltise barked, eyes flashing dangerously. "You'll only make this harder for yourself, wolf."

Tristian's gaze was intense, filled with regret, but he held firm. "It's the only way to save us both, Tyler. You can't fight this. Just trust me."

"No! I won't let you do this!" Tyler protested, trying to break free from the grip of fear. "I can fight him, we can fight together!"

"But what happens if you get hurt?" Tristian replied, desperation creeping into his tone. "You're stronger than you realize, but I won't risk your life for a chase."

"Then what about us?" Tyler asked, feeling tears pricking at the corners of his eyes. "What about everything we've fought for?"

Tristian's expression softened, pain flooding his features. "This isn't an end, it's a sacrifice. I'll come back for you. I promise. Just hold on to that, okay?"

"You can't just leave me with this monster!" Tyler was practically yelling now, his wolf snarling fiercely in his chest, yearning to break free.

Saltise interrupted, a cruel grin spreading across his face. "Time is running out, witch. What will you choose?"

"Tristian, don't do this," Tyler whispered, his heart aching as he looked towards Tristian who was staring at the ground.

"Take him.." Tristian whispered. With that Saltise stepped forwards. Tyler screamed out towards Tristian and at Stalis.

"Please" he begged before Stalis raised his hand, silencing the wolf. Swirls of magic poured out of Stalis' hand creating a magical chain. Tyler gasped as a magical collar gripped onto his neck and connected to the chain of energy.

"You will make a good pet for me boy." He spoke softly before they disappeared, Tristian refusing to make eye contact.

Soon the forest was quiet and still and Tristian let his tears fall.

"Don't worry Tyler, I'm going to save you, pet."

World Unknown

<hr>

Tyler's head throbbed as he blinked his eyes open, the world around him spinning in a blur of colors and shapes. His instincts kicked in first—the sharp awareness of danger, the unfamiliar scent in the air. He bolted upright, his muscles tensing, ready for a fight. But as his vision cleared, confusion took over. This wasn't the world he knew. The sky above him shimmered with strange hues—lavender, gold, and deep indigo swirling together like an endless sunset. The ground beneath him wasn't earth but something softer, almost like moss but glowing faintly under his touch. Trees, twisted and ancient, stretched high above, their bark etched with glowing runes that pulsed in time with his heartbeat. Where the hell am I? Tyler's heart pounded in his chest as he scanned the area, trying to remember what had happened. The last thing he recalled was Stalis—his cold, mocking smile, the sharp pain as the fairy's magic overwhelmed him. Then darkness. His blood ran cold as reality hit him. The Fae. He was in the Fae realm, an otherworldly place his kind spoke of only in warnings and legends. A place where the rules of nature didn't apply, where time twisted and bent, and where humans—and even werewolves—were nothing but pawns in the hands of its cruel inhabitants. Tyler struggled to his feet, his senses on high alert, but the world around him felt wrong. His wolf, the part of him that was always there beneath the surface, was strangely quiet, subdued in this place. He tried to reach for it, to feel the familiar pull of power that came with shifting, but it was like grasping at smoke—slipping away before he could catch hold."Great," he muttered, frustration seeping into his voice. "Just great."A soft, mocking laugh echoed from behind him, sending a shiver down his spine. He spun around, already knowing who it would be.Stalis stood a few paces away, leaning casually against one of the glowing trees, his eyes gleaming with amusement. The fairy's wings shimmered with the same eerie light as everything else in this place, and his smirk made Tyler's skin crawl."Welcome to my world, wolf," Stalis purred, his voice as smooth as silk. "I hope the journey wasn't too unpleasant."Tyler bared his teeth, his hands curling into fists. "What do you want from me?" His voice was low, dangerous, but inside he knew he was at a disadvantage. He was a stranger here, and Stalis had all the power.Stalis' grin widened as he pushed away from the tree and took a slow step closer. "Oh, don't worry," he said, his tone dripping with malice. "I have plans for you."Tyler felt his pulse quicken, but he forced himself to stay calm, to think. He couldn't let this fairy see his fear. Not here, not now.Stalis tilted his head, watching Tyler like a predator sizing up its prey. "The Fae realm is full of wonders, wolf. I'd say you're in for an unforgettable experience." He paused, eyes glinting with dark delight. "But not all of them are pleasant."Tyler's heart hammered in his chest as he braced himself for whatever was coming next. He wasn't going to go down without a fight. But in this strange, twisted world, he wasn't sure how much fight he had left."Trisitian is gonna come for me" Tyler whispered as he looked up at Stalis."Oh now, now little wolf, you think it will be that easy? When a fairy makes a deal, it is etched in stone, smeared in blood, locked into the universe. I'm sure your witch knew that though." He replied, his smile was cold, like he was playing with his food. "He couldn't have.." Tyler started as he looked at the ground trying to keep his tears from falling."Oh pet, you don't think the son of a coven leader has been warned about the deals we make?" Stalis asked sarcastically. The tall, but beautiful figure approached Tyler and lifted his head with his long fingers."Dont be sad pet.." he started."You don't get to call me that!" Tyler spat. without thinking Tyler spit in Stalis' face.The moment the spit landed on Stalis' face, time seemed to freeze. Tyler's heart skipped a beat as the air around them grew unnaturally still. Stalis blinked once, slowly, his face expressionless as he wiped the spit away with the back of his hand.Then, in the blink of an eye, the fairy's calm shattered.Stalis grabbed Tyler by the throat, his grip iron-tight as he slammed him against the nearest tree with a force that knocked the air from Tyler's lungs. The glowing runes on the tree flared violently, reacting to Stalis' fury, casting harsh light across his now twisted, rage-filled face."You insolent little worm!" Stalis hissed, his voice vibrating with barely contained rage. His beautiful features had contorted into something sharp and monstrous, his eyes glowing with a dangerous light. "Do you think you can disrespect me in my realm?"Tyler gasped for breath, his hands instinctively clawing at Stalis' wrist, but the fairy's strength was inhuman. His grip tightened, cutting off Tyler's air, the world around him starting to blur."You filthy mutt," Stalis growled, his voice low and deadly. "You think your pathetic wolf pack or little witch boyfriend can save you here? You are nothing. No one comes for you in the realm of the Fae. No one dares to challenge me." His wings flared out behind him, their sharp edges glittering like deadly blades in the strange light.Tyler's vision darkened at the edges, but he refused to show fear. His wolf was buried deep, caged in this place, but his spirit wasn't broken yet. He managed to force out a defiant glare, his chest heaving as he tried to breathe against the crushing pressure on his throat.Stalis leaned in closer, his breath hot and filled with barely controlled fury. "You'll learn your place here," he hissed. "I could break you in an instant, wolf. Tear your soul apart and feed it to the shadows. But that would be too easy, wouldn't it?"Tyler felt a cold chill snake through him at Stalis' words, but he held his ground, even as black spots danced in his vision."No," Stalis continued, his voice dropping to a dangerous whisper, "I think I'll take my time with you. I'll make you beg for death, and when you finally break..." He smiled again, a cruel, twisted smile. "...I'll be the one to decide if you're worth saving."With a final, vicious squeeze, Stalis released Tyler, letting him crumple to the ground in a coughing, gasping heap. Tyler clutched at his throat, choking on air as he tried to steady himself, his body trembling from the violent encounter.Stalis stood over him, the fury in his eyes slowly fading back into cold amusement. "Remember your place, wolf," he sneered. "You're mine now. There's no escaping it."Tyler coughed, his throat raw, but he forced himself to look up at Stalis, fire still burning in his chest despite the pain. He wasn't going to give this fairy the satisfaction of seeing him broken. Not yet.Stalis narrowed his eyes, then turned on his heel, his wings folding behind him as he walked away, leaving Tyler on the glowing, mossy ground. "We'll see how long that defiance lasts," he called over his shoulder, his voice dripping with malice.Tyler lay there, gasping for breath, his mind spinning as he tried to regain control. He didn't know how he'd survive this, but one thing was clear—Stalis wasn't just malicious; he was far more dangerous than Tyler had ever imagined. And now, Tyler was trapped in his world."I can be good to you Tyler, we don't have to be enemies, but I will not tolerate this behavior. It's not fair that you and that... that witch," He said in disgust "Get to have an unnatural bond while us fairies cant even mate with pathetic humans without being hunted like deer. We can be friends Tyler, I can give you everything you dreamed of. A home, all the food you can eat. No more being used as pawns in other peoples games, no more hiding behind your father, no more being tortured by your filthy pack of mutts who don't even care about you.Stalis crochet down next to Tyler and brushed his cheek. Tyler started ahead, still rubbing his throat."How do you know all that?" Tyler asked quietly, refusing to look at Stalis.Stalis stopped before his smile turned into embarrassment. "I've been watching you for sometime Tyler...every tear you shed, every scream you screamed from the top of your lungs out of anger. I've been watching you for quite some time..always in the shadows. Waiting for the day that I could take you, save you. It was all ruined when that pathetic witch showed up and got to play hero." Stalis continued visibly angry at even mentioning Tristian. "And then he goes and bonds you together?" he asked, standing up and turning around, trying not to show his anger. He stopped talking and stared towards the off-colored sky. "Oh how quickly those bonds broke.." he said with a small chuckle.Tyler felt a chill crawl up his spine as Stalis spoke. The idea that the fairy had been watching him for so long, lurking in the shadows, filled him with an unsettling dread. The way Stalis said "saving" him didn't feel like rescue—it felt like a trap, like chains disguised as promises.He swallowed hard, his throat still sore from the earlier assault. His mind raced, trying to make sense of Stalis' words, of the deep resentment and obsession that seemed to seethe just beneath his calm surface."You think you can save me?" Tyler asked, his voice hoarse, but there was defiance in his eyes now. He finally looked at Stalis, no longer willing to cower. "By tearing me away from my world? By ripping me out of my life and dragging me into... this?" He gestured around at the twisted Fae realm, the unnatural beauty tainted by an undercurrent of danger.Stalis' back remained turned, his body tense as he gazed at the strange sky. "Your world is broken, Tyler," he replied, his voice softer now but still simmering with anger. "You've spent your whole life being used. By your pack, by your family, by your so-called friends. Even by him." His voice dripped with venom at the mention of Tristian. "And yet, you defend them. Why? Why stay loyal to those who've done nothing but hurt you?"Tyler clenched his jaw, the pain in his throat paling in comparison to the emotional weight of Stalis' words. Part of him wanted to argue, to tell Stalis he was wrong, that his pack did care about him, that Tristian hadn't used him. But another part of him—the part still stinging from all the betrayals and the loneliness—hesitated."I'm not yours to save," Tyler said after a long pause, his voice quiet but resolute. "Whatever you think you're offering me... it's not real. It's just another cage."Stalis whirled around, eyes flashing with a mix of hurt and fury. "Not real?" he spat, stepping closer to Tyler, his wings flaring slightly. "What is real then, Tyler? That pack you cling to? That bond with your witch that's already fading? Look around!" He spread his arms wide, his voice rising with emotion. "This world, my world, is more real than anything you've ever known. I can give you freedom here, away from the wolves that despise you and the magic that binds you."Tyler stared up at him, heart hammering in his chest. He could see the cracks forming in Stalis' carefully controlled demeanor. Beneath the malice, there was something desperate, something broken. The anger wasn't just rage—it was pain."You don't get it, do you?" Tyler said, his voice low but steady. "You talk about freedom, but you've been hiding in the shadows, obsessed with me, with whatever you think I am. That's not freedom, Stalis. That's being trapped in your own bitterness."Stalis' face twisted, a flash of pure fury crossing his features as he stepped even closer, his presence overwhelming. Tyler could feel the heat of his breath, the sharp intensity of his gaze."Careful, wolf," Stalis growled, his voice laced with barely contained rage. "I've been merciful so far. But you're testing my patience."Tyler didn't flinch. "I'm not afraid of you," he said, though his heart raced as he spoke the words. "You can take me away from my world, but you'll never control me. Not like that."For a moment, Stalis stood there, trembling with fury, his fists clenched at his sides. The fairy's wings twitched, and his eyes burned with the dark fire of barely restrained violence. Tyler braced himself, expecting another outburst, but instead, Stalis took a step back, his expression hardening into something cold and unreadable."You'll learn, Tyler," he said softly, his voice like ice. "You'll learn that no one can save you from me—not your pack, not your witch, and not even yourself."With that, Stalis turned on his heel, his wings folding neatly behind him as he strode away, disappearing into the shadows of the Fae realm, leaving Tyler alone in the strange, glowing landscape. But even as the fairy vanished, his presence lingered like a dark cloud over Tyler's heart.Tyler sat there, rubbing his throat, the weight of everything pressing down on him. The chain around him glowed. Tyler sat on the soft grass trying to reach through the bond, not that he would even know how. Everytime he tried he only grew more upset as he got nothing in return. "Tristian... Where are you?" he spoke out loud before erupting into tears as he laid on the soft grass.***"Tristian knelt in the middle of his spell circle, the flickering candlelight casting sharp shadows across his face. His brow was furrowed in concentration, beads of sweat forming along his hairline as he chanted the ancient words. Around him, the air crackled with raw magic, swirling like a storm about to break. Runes etched into the floor glowed faintly beneath his fingertips, pulsing in rhythm with his heartbeat.But something was wrong.The energy, once vibrant and responsive to his call, began to dissipate, slipping through his fingers like sand. He gritted his teeth, his voice growing louder as he forced more power into the incantation."Obsecro portam aperiri! Audi me! Via ad Fae pandere!" His voice rang out, desperate and commanding, but the words hung in the air, heavy and unheeded.The circle trembled slightly, the runes flickering as if they were losing their connection to the magic of the Fae realm. Tristian's heart raced as he slammed his hand against the ground, pouring everything he had into the spell. He couldn't fail. Not now."Come on!" he hissed through gritted teeth, his hands trembling with the strain. His connection to Tyler felt distant, the bond weakening more with every passing hour. He had to find him—had to pull him out of that world. The thought of Tyler trapped there, alone, with him—with Stalis—was unbearable.The circle flashed brightly for a moment, a brief surge of hope flickering in his chest. But then, as quickly as it came, the light dimmed and the air stilled. The magic sputtered out, and the runes beneath him dulled to nothing.Tristian collapsed to his knees, his breath ragged, frustration and exhaustion weighing heavily on him. He slammed his fist into the ground, growling in frustration. "Damn it!"For days now, he had been trying—every spell, every ritual, every ancient invocation he could find—but the Fae world remained locked, sealed tight against his magic. It was as though the realm itself was actively rejecting him, mocking his attempts to break through."Why won't it work?" he muttered to himself, his voice cracking with anger and fear. "Why can't I get to him?"The candle flames flickered as a gust of wind swept through the room, snuffing them out one by one. Darkness settled over the space, leaving only the faintest glow of the spent runes beneath him. Tristian's heart sank as the weight of failure pressed down on him.He had been so sure this time. The old times had promised a way into the Fae realm, a passage through the veil, but each attempt brought him nothing but resistance. His bond with Tyler, once a lifeline that could have guided him, now felt frayed and distant, like trying to grasp a ghost.Tristian's hands shook as he rubbed them over his face, his mind racing. He couldn't give up. Tyler was out there, somewhere, trapped in a world that twisted everything it touched. And Stalis, with his twisted obsession, would make sure Tyler suffered if he wasn't already.He stood abruptly, knocking over one of the extinguished candles as he paced in the dark. His heart was heavy with guilt, knowing that his failure might cost Tyler everything. He wasn't just trapped—he was vulnerable. And Tristian had promised him he'd always be there."Damn it, Tyler..." Tristian whispered, his voice breaking. "I'm coming. I swear, I'm coming for you ."But even as he said the words, doubt gnawed at him. The Fae realm was beyond his reach, beyond his magic, and every second he wasted brought Tyler closer to whatever fate Stalis had planned.He clenched his fists, his nails digging into his palms until they hurt. There had to be another way. Another spell. Another source of magic. He would tear apart every ancient grimoire, search through every forgotten legend if he had to. He wasn't going to lose Tyler to that monster.With renewed determination, Tristian turned toward the shelves lining the walls, packed with books and scrolls, some so old they looked ready to crumble. He needed something—anything—that would break through the barrier between worlds. If his magic wasn't enough, he'd find a way to make it enough.As he pulled an old, dust-covered tome from the shelf, flipping through its brittle pages, a single thought echoed in his mind.Hold on, Tyler. Just hold on

Mending Deals

Tristian gazed up at the night sky, the stars distant and indifferent to his pain. Every spell, every incantation he tried had failed, leaving him drained and desperate. His once-sacred books and carefully laid-out tools now felt like worthless relics of a power he no longer commanded. His chest tightened with the weight of helplessness, his hope crumbling to dust.

Tears streamed down his face, hot and relentless, as the crushing guilt took hold. This is my fault, he thought bitterly. I should have protected him. The memory of Tyler's abduction haunted him, replaying endlessly in his mind. He had failed him.

"Mom!" he cried out, the word ripping from his throat, raw and broken. It felt pathetic, like the call of a child who should have grown beyond such desperation. "Anyone..." His voice cracked as he collapsed to his knees, fists clenched. "God, Hecate... anyone, please!" His voice was hoarse, his plea lost to the vast, uncaring night.

He stared at the sky, his red, swollen eyes searching for a sign, but all he found was silence. The universe remained cold and unyielding, leaving

Tristian to drown in his own grief, his once-mighty magic feeling as fragile as the tears that streaked down his puffy cheeks.

Soon leaves started to rustle, the wind howling. Tristian's mother appeared in a swirl of shimmering light, her form coalescing from the moonlit mist that surrounded him. She was a vision of ethereal beauty, her long hair flowing like liquid silver, and her robes glimmered with the essence of stars. The air crackled with magic as she descended, her presence both calming and powerful.

"Tristian," she said, her voice a melodic whisper that cut through his despair. "Why do you call for me in such anguish?"

He looked up, tears blurring his vision, his heart aching at the sight of her. "Mom, I... I couldn't save him. Tyler is gone, taken by the fae, and I don't know how to get him back."

She knelt beside him, her gaze steady and reassuring. "You carry the weight of your power and your failures, but do not forget that you are not alone. There is a way to enter the fae realm, but it comes with great risk."

Tristian looked at his mother, frustration boiling over as he struggled to comprehend the situation. "I don't understand why I can't get through," he asked, his voice thick with desperation. "I've tried every spell I know. Why won't they let me into the fae realm?"

His mother's gaze softened, her eyes filled with understanding. "It's not as simple as casting a spell, Tristian. If you make a deal with a fairy, only they can find you to remake the deal. They are bound by their own rules, and once a pact is made, it can only be renewed by the one you negotiated with."

"But that doesn't make sense!" he protested, frustration and anguish mingling. Why keep me from reaching him?"

"They thrive on chaos and power, my son. To them, you are just another pawn in their game. They revel in the pain and suffering of others," she explained, her voice steady and calm, a stark contrast to his turmoil. "But if you can capture one of their own, you can bend their will. It's the only way to break through their barriers and find Tyler."

With her words echoing in his mind, Tristian felt a rush of determination. He would face the peril of trapping a fairy, no matter how dangerous it might be. Tyler was worth every risk. "I'll do whatever it takes," he vowed, his heart pounding with renewed resolve.

His mother nodded, a flicker of pride lighting her expression. "Remember, Tristian, trust in your instincts and your magic. You are stronger than you realize. Now go, and may the moonlight guide your path."

As she began to fade, the mist surrounding her shimmered like stardust, leaving Tristian with the lingering warmth of her presence and the weight of his mission ahead. He wiped his tears and took a deep breath.Tristian knelt on the cool grass, the moon hanging high in the sky like a watchful guardian. Its silvery light bathed the landscape, illuminating the shadows that danced around him. He took a deep breath, trying to calm the storm within him as he focused on the task at hand. Summoning a fairy was no small feat; he needed to be clever and resourceful.

He thought back to the old texts, the whispers of spells he'd overheard during coven meetings, and the stories of how other witches had succeeded—or failed—in dealing with the fae. His mind raced, piecing together fragments of knowledge that danced at the edges of his memory.

"Their vanity... their greed," he muttered to himself, recalling tales of how fairies were often drawn to shiny objects or promises of power. "A trap... something irresistible to lure them in."

He glanced around, scanning the ground for any items he could use. Just to the side, he spotted a glimmering shard of glass, reflecting the moonlight like a fallen star. It would work as bait, he decided. The fae were known to be drawn to beauty and sparkle. With that in mind, he needed a powerful spell to weave the trap—something that would not only attract the fairy but also bind it to his will.

"Let's see," Tristian murmured, closing his eyes as he let the energy of the moon flow through him. He began to visualize the incantation, weaving together the ancient words he'd learned from his mother. "I need to anchor the spell... create a circle for the binding."

He envisioned the circle—a sacred boundary that would trap the fairy once it was lured close enough. The more he concentrated, the clearer it became in his mind. "I'll need salt... and a few petals from the moonflower and a shard of glass," he said aloud, his heart racing at the thought of actually performing the spell. The moonflower would amplify the enchantment, enhancing its potency.

Tristian took one last glance at the moon, feeling its pull and power surging within him. "This is it," he whispered, a mixture of fear and determination coursing through his veins. "I will find you, Tyler. I won't give up on you."

He set to work, gathering the materials he needed to prepare the trap. Each step was infused with intention as he drew the circle in the dirt, laying down the salt and petals with care. He set the glass on the stump of a tree towards the circle and under the moon. As he arranged everything, he felt the weight of the world upon his shoulders—yet the moonlight gave him strength, reminding him of his purpose. This was his chance to rescue Tyler from the clutches of Stalis.

With his makeshift trap prepared, Tristian took a deep breath, centering himself as he knelt within the circle he'd drawn. The moon's glow intensified, casting a silvery hue over his materials—a shard of glass, salt, and moonflower petals. He could feel the energy of the night surging around him, amplifying his resolve.

"Here goes nothing," he murmured, his heart pounding with anticipation and fear.

He clasped his hands together, closing his eyes as he focused on the power flowing through him. He could visualize the essence of the fae, their beauty and trickery, and he poured his energy into the incantation he had prepared. As he began to speak, he felt the vibrations of the words resonate deep within his soul.

"Luceo et captus, et cum splendor venire, Fae, audite me, in umbra et lumine. In hoc circulo, tenete, non evadere, Vincula mea, signa, veritate tradere."

The Latin rolled off his tongue, the syllables wrapping around him like a protective shroud. Each word ignited the air, shimmering with magic, causing the ground beneath him to pulse in response.

As he finished the incantation, he opened his eyes, the glass shard catching the moonlight and sending shards of illumination scattering across the yard. Tristian felt a rush of energy coursing through him as the air around him began to thrum with anticipation. He kept his focus on the shard, willing it to attract the fairy, using its radiant beauty as bait.

A gentle breeze stirred, and Tristian's heart raced as he sensed the faintest shift in the air, as if something—or someone—was drawn to the circle. He held his breath, waiting, each moment stretching into eternity. Then, just at the edge of his vision, he saw a flicker of light, dancing and shimmering like a star come to life.

"Please, let this work," he whispered, a mix of hope and desperation swirling within him. The shimmering light darted closer, swirling around the circle with an almost playful energy. Tristian could feel the tension build, the anticipation crackling like static electricity in the air.

The fairy, caught by the glint of the glass, hovered just outside the boundary, momentarily mesmerized. Tristian's heart raced as he prepared for the final part of his plan. With a deep breath, he stepped forward, extending his hand toward the glowing figure. "You're mine now," he declared, ready to bind the fairy and forge a path to rescue Tyler.

As the shimmering light approached, Tristian's heart pounded louder in his ears. The fairy materialized before him, revealing a breathtaking figure—a beautiful man dressed in a flowing black tunic that contrasted starkly with his luminous skin. Delicate features framed by tousled hair caught the moonlight, making him look ethereal. However, one of his wings was broken, hanging limply at his side, a reminder of the fragility of his kind.

The fairy hovered just within the circle, eyes wide and shimmering with curiosity, yet laced with caution. Tristian felt a surge of compassion mixed with determination. He couldn't allow the creature's beauty to distract him; he had to act swiftly.

"Fae, te detineo, hac vincula impero, In hac lucida nocte, te alligo! Non fugies, non evades, per potestatem meam, Hanc pactum serva, quam cerno, quam creabo."

As he spoke the incantation, the circle began to glow fiercely, casting radiant beams of light that intertwined around the fairy. Tristian felt the power of the words surge through him, wrapping the fairy in an invisible binding force that pulsed with energy.

The fairy's eyes widened in realization, and he attempted to retreat, but the glow intensified, trapping him within the circle. "You cannot hold me!" he exclaimed, his voice a melodic blend of anger and desperation. He struggled against the binding light, but it wrapped tighter around him like vines, anchoring him in place.

"Just a moment," Tristian replied, his voice steadier than he felt. "I need your help. I'll set you free, but you must take me to the Fae realm. My friend is in danger."

The fairy's expression shifted, a mixture of defiance and intrigue. "You think you can bargain with me?" he challenged, his voice soft yet firm.

"I can give you your freedom," Tristian replied earnestly. "But I need your word to take me to Tyler. Please."

"The only way I can take you to my realm is if we make a deal," the fairy said through gritted teeth, his eyes flashing with irritation and a hint of longing for freedom.

Tristian nodded, his heart racing. "A deal," he echoed, trying to keep his voice steady despite the gravity of the situation. "What are the terms?"

The fairy's gaze intensified, a mixture of challenge and intrigue sparking between them. "You must promise to mend my broken wing in exchange for your passage. Only then can I take you to the Fae realm."

Tristian's breath caught in his throat as he considered the request. He had never worked with fairy magic before, let alone attempted to heal a creature from that realm. "I... I can do that," he said hesitantly, though doubt crept into his mind.

The fairy narrowed his eyes, assessing Tristian. "You must swear to heal my wing, no matter the cost. If you fail, you'll be trapped in the Fae realm forever."

"I promise," Tristian said, determination rising within him. "I'll fix your wing as soon as we arrive."

"Swear it by the magic that binds you," the fairy insisted, the glow of the circle shimmering around him like a cage of light. "Your word must be binding."

"I swear by the magic of my ancestors and the power of this circle," Tristian declared, his voice unwavering. "I will mend your wing in exchange for my passage."

The fairy studied Tristian's face, searching for any hint of deceit. Satisfied, he nodded slightly. "Very well. We have a deal," he said, his tone softening, though still laced with a hint of wariness. "Now, you must let me go."

With a wave of his hand, Tristian felt the binding spell shift slightly, allowing the fairy to move freely within the circle while still being contained. "What do I need to do to summon your power?" Tristian asked, desperation mingling with anticipation.

"Speak the words of invitation, and the doorway will open," the fairy replied, his voice now smooth and melodic, as if the tension had loosened slightly. "But know this: once you step into my realm, the dangers that await you are beyond your imagination."

Tristian inhaled deeply, determination surging through him. "I'm ready. I'll do whatever it takes to save Tyler."

The fairy's expression shifted, a flicker of admiration crossing his features. "Very well. Repeat after me: "Fata lucida, aperi nobis portam, ad regnum Fae."

Tristian echoed the incantation, the words rolling off his tongue like an ancient melody. The air around them began to shimmer, vibrating with energy as the boundary between realms thinned.

"Now, we will cross together," the fairy instructed, his demeanor shifting from wary to commanding. "Hold on to your resolve, for the Fae realm is a place of beauty and danger."

As the words resonated in the night air, a swirling portal of light began to open before them, revealing glimpses of an enchanting world beyond—one filled with vibrant colors, strange flora, and shadows that danced just out of sight. With a determined nod, Tristian stepped forward, ready to face whatever awaited him in the Fae realm to rescue Tyler.

Tristian took in his surroundings, still adjusting to the overwhelming sensations of the Fae realm. Aelith, who had remained silent until now, stepped forward with a graceful, almost regal air.

"I suppose introductions are in order," Aelith said, his voice smooth but with a hint of impatience. "I am Aelith, of the Water Court. While I'm not your guide through the Fae realm, I have brought you this far. Now that we're here—" He gestured to the shimmering world around them, his tone shifting to something more serious. "—it's time for you to fulfill your promise."

Tristian nodded, recalling their earlier agreement. "Right. You want me to fix your wing."

Aelith's eyes narrowed slightly as he revealed his delicate, shimmering wing, bent at an odd angle. "Yes. You're going to fix it."

"Um... I'm glad that you got me here, but how exactly can I fix your wing? Can't you do it since you're a fairy?" Tristian asked, examining the wing closely. The delicate membranes shimmered in the ethereal light, but the way it was bent hinted at a deeper injury.

Aelith's expression turned serious, his gaze unwavering. "No, I cannot. This damage was caused by a witch's spell, one that even the most skilled fairies of the Water Court cannot undo. The magic that binds my wing requires a witch's touch to mend."

Tristian furrowed his brow, uncertainty creeping in. "But I've never done anything like this before. What if I mess it up?"

Aelith stepped closer, his voice dropping to a soothing tone. "You will not mess it up. I believe in your ability. Trust yourself and focus. Just follow my instructions, and we can both get what we want."

"Okay, right, I'll just, uh..." Tristian started, searching his mind for a spell that might mend Aelith's wing. The remnants of his magical training flickered in his thoughts, but uncertainty gnawed at him. He had only ever practiced minor charms, nothing as intricate as healing a broken wing.

Aelith watched him intently, his expression a mix of encouragement and impatience. "Focus, Tristian. Think of what you know about healing magic. You've got this."

Tristian closed his eyes for a moment, drawing in a deep breath. He could feel the magic around him, shimmering and alive, but he needed to channel it. "Okay," he muttered to himself. "Maybe if I combine a healing spell with the energy from the Water Court..."

He opened his eyes, determination replacing doubt. "I think I have an idea. Just... hold still."

Aelith nodded, his gaze steady. "I'm ready. Just remember, you have to visualize the magic flowing through you and into my wing."

"This might be a dumb question, but can I even use magic here?" Tristian asked, hesitating as he touched Aelith's wing. The delicate surface felt cool and smooth beneath his fingers, but doubt crept in. "I don't know how this world works."

Aelith met his gaze, his expression reassuring. "You can use magic here, but it will be different than in your world. The Fae realm amplifies magic, but it also demands precision. Trust your instincts, and the energy will respond to you."

Tristian nodded, trying to absorb Aelith's words. He took a deep breath, centering himself as he focused on the magic coursing around them. "Okay. I'll give it a try."

As he concentrated, he could feel the pulsating energy of the realm resonating with his own magic, weaving through him like a gentle stream. With newfound confidence, he closed his eyes again, channeling his intent toward Aelith's wing.

Tristian closed his eyes and focused, feeling the energy around him pulse in rhythm with his heartbeat. He envisioned Aelith's wing mending, the delicate membranes healing under the warmth of his magic. As the words formed in his mind, he spoke them aloud, weaving his intent into the incantation:

"O waters deep, and shadows long, Heed my call, awaken strong. Undo now a witch's wrong, By winter's day and nights of long.

By moon's grace and starlit veil, Let healing flow, let darkness pale. Ancient bonds of earth and sky, Reforge the wing, let magic fly.

With the whispers of the Fae, Restore the light, bring forth the day."

As he recited the spell, Tristian visualized a soft blue glow surrounding Aelith's wing, pulling the torn edges together and weaving them back into place. He reached deep within himself, drawing on the energy of the Fae realm to strengthen his magic.

As Tristian recited the final line of the spell, a soft blue glow enveloped Aelith's wing, illuminating the darkness around them. The air shimmered with energy, and the very essence of the Fae realm seemed to respond to his call.

Aelith gasped softly as the glow intensified, and the veins within his wing began to shimmer, flowing like water beneath the surface. The broken parts, once twisted and fragile, started to mend before Tristian's eyes.

With each pulse of magic, the delicate membranes reformed, knitting together with a grace that mirrored the fluidity of water. Aelith's wing quivered, the light cascading through it, reflecting hues of blue and silver as the injury healed.

"Keep going," Aelith urged, his voice steady but filled with awe. "You're doing it!"

Tristian concentrated harder, pouring his energy into the spell, willing it to take hold. The connection between them deepened, the magic intertwining with Aelith's essence. The glow brightened further, illuminating the space around them, and with one final surge, the last remnants of the injury faded away.

Aelith flexed his wing, the movement fluid and powerful, and a smile broke across his face. "You did it! My wing... it's whole again!"

Aelith smiled at Tristian as he flapped his wings, testing their restored strength. "Thank you so much," he said, looking at Tristian with gratitude before embracing him. "I know our deal is done, but as a token of appreciation, I'd like to assist you further. Whom do you seek?"

Tristian returned the smile, feeling a sense of camaraderie with the fairy. "I'm searching for my friend Tyler. A fairy named Stalis has taken him, and I need to find them."

Aelith's expression darkened, concern flashing across his face. "Stalis..." he murmured, his tone laced with warning. "He's not just any fairy—he's a prince of the Fire Court."

Tristian's eyes widened in shock. "A prince?"

"Yes," Aelith nodded gravely. "The Fire Court is powerful, and they take whatever they want, so long as it isn't already claimed by another court. Stalis, in particular, is known for his cruelty and ambition. He thrives on deceit and malice. If he has your friend, it won't be easy to get him back."

Tristian felt a pit form in his stomach. "But I have to try. Tyler's my friend... I can't leave him with someone like that. We have to find him"

Tristian felt a pit form in his stomach. "But I have to try. Tyler's my friend... I can't leave him with someone like that." His voice wavered for a moment before hardening with determination. "We need to save him."

Aelith's eyes widened in surprise, fear flickering across his face as he took a step back. "We?" His voice was low, almost a whisper, as though the very mention of it brought danger closer. "Stalis kills anything in his way if he thinks he owns it. I'm not going anywhere near the South Lands. That place is a death trap."

Tristian's resolve faltered for a moment at the intensity of Aelith's reaction. He hadn't realized just how dangerous this journey would be, but the thought of Tyler trapped in Stalis's grasp pushed him forward. "I can't do this alone, Aelith. I need your help."

Aelith shook his head, his wings trembling slightly as he turned away, staring into the distance. "You don't understand. The Fire Court takes what they want, and Stalis is ruthless. The South Lands are nothing but barren wastelands of ash and fire. I barely escaped there with my life once... I won't go back."

Tristian's desperation surged, and he stepped closer to Aelith, his voice lowering to a pleading whisper. "Please, Aelith. I need your help. Tyler is in danger, and I can't do this alone. You know the Fae realm better than I do. I can't lose him."

Aelith shook his head vehemently, his wings twitching nervously. "You don't understand the risks, Tristian! Stalis is not just powerful; he's merciless. I can't go back there. I won't!"

Frustration boiled inside Tristian. "But you owe me for fixing your wing! I did what I promised, and now you have to help me. You know I can't leave Tyler with him!"

Aelith's expression turned wary as he sensed the shift in Tristian's demeanor. "You wouldn't..."

Tristian stepped back, his jaw tightening. "I could break your wing again, Aelith. Technically, our deal was completed when you were healed. I could do it without a second thought."

Aelith's eyes widened in shock and fear. "You wouldn't dare!" he gasped, backing away, his wings instinctively fluttering as if trying to escape the threat.

Tristian's voice was steady but filled with determination. "I will if it means saving my friend! This isn't just about you anymore. Tyler's life is at stake."

Aelith sighed heavily, his shoulders slumping in defeat. "Fine. I'll help you," he said reluctantly, his voice barely above a whisper. "But understand, this doesn't come without its own dangers. I can't promise we'll succeed."

Tristian felt a rush of relief mixed with the weight of the looming peril. "Thank you, Aelith. I'll do whatever it takes to make this work."

Aelith's gaze turned serious as he looked at Tristian. "We must be careful. The Fire Court will not hesitate to destroy anyone who threatens their claim."

Tristian felt a rush of relief wash over him as Aelith reluctantly agreed to help. The weight of uncertainty still lingered, but he now had a partner in this perilous journey.

"Thank you, Aelith. I'll do whatever it takes to make this work," he said, his voice steady with resolve.

Aelith nodded, though his expression remained troubled. "We must be careful. The Fire Court will not hesitate to destroy anyone who threatens their claim. Stalis will not be easily thwarted."

With a shared understanding of the danger that lay ahead, they began to prepare for their journey. Aelith led Tristian deeper into the Fae realm, the air thick with magic and tension. Shadows flickered at the edges of their vision, reminding them of the lurking threats that awaited them in the South Lands.

As they moved through the vibrant yet ominous forest, Tristian's thoughts were solely focused on Tyler, driving him forward with a fierce determination. He would not let his wold face Stalis alone.

Forging Alliances

✱ **Hello all! As I say in all of my books, please make sure to like and comment. I love taking suggestions or thoughts on where you would like to see this story go!***

Celeste strode into the heart of Baxtrail territory, her head held high, though her magic hummed with tension. The air between witches and wolves had always been thick with hostility, and today was no different. The guards barely masked their disdain as they let her pass, but Celeste paid them no mind. Her focus was on Marcus—the alpha.

Marcus stood at the center of the room, arms crossed, his powerful frame exuding authority. He didn't bother to hide his suspicion as his piercing eyes landed on Celeste.

"Witch," he growled, his tone flat and cold. "What do you want?"

"I'm not here by choice, Marcus," Celeste replied coolly, meeting his gaze. "It's about your son."

At that, Marcus stiffened. "What about Tyler?"

Celeste drew a breath, steadying herself before she spoke. "He's been taken. To the Fae realm."

The silence that followed her words was suffocating. Marcus's eyes narrowed dangerously, his muscles tensing as if ready to strike. "The Fae realm?" he repeated, disbelief lacing his voice. "What the hell do you mean by that?"

"Exactly what it sounds like," Celeste said, her tone sharp. "Tristian was trying to help, but it didn't go as planned. He made a deal with a fairy, and now Tyler has been taken into their world."

Marcus's growl shook the air around them. "Your son made a deal with a fairy, and my son gets dragged into the Fae realm? Do you even know what you've done?"

"What I've done?" Celeste's eyes flared with anger. "This wasn't my doing, Marcus. Tristian tried to fix the situation before it spiraled. But the Fae don't play fair—you should know that better than anyone. And now Tyler's gone because of their tricks."

Marcus's fists clenched at his sides, his teeth bared in a snarl. "You let your son meddle in affairs he doesn't understand. You witches always think you can control everything—"

"And you wolves always think you can tear through every problem with brute force," Celeste snapped back. "This isn't about control. It's about getting your son back before the Fae do something worse."

Marcus stepped closer, his fury palpable. "And how, exactly, are you planning on doing that? You don't even know who took him, do you?"

"I don't," Celeste admitted, her voice tight. "But Tristian is already trying to find a way to get Tyler back. He's crossed into their realm—he's our only chance of retrieving your son."

Marcus let out a harsh laugh, but there was no humor in it. "So I'm supposed to just trust that your son, the one who got Tyler into this mess, is going to save him? That's a joke, Celeste. One that could cost my son his life."

"You think I don't know the stakes here?" Celeste's voice dropped, a dangerous edge creeping in. "This isn't about trust, Marcus. It's about doing what needs to be done. If you have a better option, I'd love to hear it. But right now, Tristian is all we have."

The two leaders stared each other down, the tension crackling between them like a storm on the verge of breaking. Marcus's breathing was heavy, his wolf instincts screaming to take action, but there was nothing he could do—not in the Fae realm. And Celeste, for all her icy demeanor, was right.

"You better pray your son knows what he's doing," Marcus growled. "Because if anything happens to Tyler, there'll be hell to pay."

Celeste's expression hardened. "I already know the cost, Marcus. But we don't have time for threats. The longer Tyler stays in the Fae realm, the more dangerous it becomes. I'm here to tell you what's happening—not to ask for your permission."

Marcus's eyes burned with fury, but he didn't argue. He knew, as much as he hated to admit it, that Celeste was right. The wolves couldn't reach into the Fae realm; they didn't understand its twisted rules and magic. And if Tristian was already there, then he was the best hope they had.

"Fine," Marcus muttered through gritted teeth. "But if your boy fails, it's not just him who will suffer. You can bet on that."

Celeste nodded, her face cold and composed. "Then let's hope he doesn't."

***

Tyler's eyelids fluttered as he slowly emerged from unconsciousness, his body sinking into the softest surface he had ever felt. The room was warm, a strange comfort in contrast to the uneasy feeling stirring within him. He blinked a few times, his eyes adjusting to the soft, golden light that filled the space.

As his vision cleared, the grandeur of the room around him came into focus. The walls were made of smooth, polished stone that shimmered with a subtle iridescence, catching the glow from large chandeliers overhead. Rich tapestries of deep burgundy and gold draped elegantly from the walls, each depicting scenes of Fae royalty and magic in vibrant detail. The bed he lay on was massive, surrounded by silken sheets in shades of crimson and orange, the fabric cool and luxurious against his skin.

Tyler's heart raced as the reality of where he was settled in—he was no longer in the human world. The beauty of the room felt suffocating, as if its elegance was meant to distract him from the sinister game at play. His muscles tensed, but before he could fully gather his bearings, the door to the room creaked open.

Standing in the doorway was Stalis.

The fairy prince glided into the room, his presence commanding as ever. His outfit shimmered in the light—silk robes of fiery orange and red that clung to his graceful frame, every movement a dance of vibrant colors. The silks swayed as he moved, like flames licking the air, perfectly tailored to showcase his dangerous beauty. His golden eyes sparkled with mischief, lips curling into a knowing smile as he approached Tyler.

"Good, you're awake," Stalis said, his voice smooth as silk, matching the opulence of the room. He stopped beside the bed, his gaze never leaving Tyler's face. "I was wondering how long you would sleep. But I suppose you needed the rest."

Tyler sat up, the sheets slipping from his bare chest. "Where am I?" His voice was hoarse, the tension rising in his throat.

Stalis chuckled, a low and melodic sound. "You're in my palace, of course. The Fire Court. I thought it fitting to give you somewhere... comfortable, while you adjust to your new surroundings."

Tyler's eyes darted around the room, trying to understand the scope of his situation. "Why am I here? What do you want with me?"

Stalis reached out, tracing a finger along the edge of the bedpost. "All in due time, wolf. For now, consider yourself my guest. I have plans for you, but there's no need to rush. After all, we're in the realm of the Fae—time flows differently here."

The fairy prince's words were laced with amusement, but Tyler didn't miss the underlying threat. This wasn't a rescue, nor was it an invitation. He was here at Stalis's whim, and his freedom felt more distant than ever.

Tyler's jaw tightened. "I'm not your pet."

Stalis's smile widened, eyes gleaming with firelight. "We'll see about that."

"See about what?" Tyler retorted, pulling himself up to sit at the edge of the bed. He wasn't about to let the fairy feel powerful in this situation. "What do you think is going to happen here?"

Stalis stepped forward, his presence overwhelming yet tantalizing. "You misunderstand, dear Tyler. You're not a prisoner. You're a valuable asset in this grand scheme I'm orchestrating." He paused, allowing his words to sink in. "And you were meant to play a pivotal role."

"A role?" Tyler echoed, his heart pounding with a mixture of fear and indignation. "I don't want to be part of your schemes. Just let me go.""

Stalis feigned a thoughtful look, tilting his head with intrigue. "Oh, but that's where you're mistaken. You see, the Fae realm has its rules, and once you're here, it's not quite so simple to l Tyler spoke soft as he looked up towards Stalis.eave. You will find I can make your existence... very enjoyable." His voice was dripping with charm, though the underlying threat weighed heavily in the air.

I'd rather be in a cell than your 'guest'," Tyler shot back, his defiance igniting a fire within him. "You think you can charm your way into convincing me to stay?"

Stalis laughed lightly, his golden eyes glinting with unabashed delight. "Oh, darling wolf, it's not about charm. You'll come to see things from my perspective eventually.

"Tristian will come for me.."

talis raised an eyebrow, the amusement never leaving his expression. "Tristian, is it? How quaint. You believe he'll just march in here, guns blazing, and rescue you? This is my realm, and I assure you, he'll have his work cut out for him."

Tyler's heart sank at the thought, but he held his ground. "He will come for me," he insisted, the conviction in his voice surprising even himself. "You have no idea what he's capable of."

"Ah, but that's where you underestimate the Fae," Stalis replied, his tone playful yet laced with menace. "You see, while your precious Tristian plays the hero, I'll be one step ahead. You're in a game far beyond your understanding, and I control the board."

"Is that so?" Tyler challenged, anger flaring within him. "What makes you think I'll just roll over and play along with your little game?"

Stalis stepped closer, his presence intoxicating yet suffocating. "Because, dear wolf, you'll soon realize that resisting is not only futile but... rather painful." His voice lowered, a seductive whisper that sent chills down Tyler's spine. "I can make your stay here... quite pleasurable, but I can also make it a nightmare. The choice is yours."

Tyler shivered, the implications of Stalis's words hanging heavily in the air. He needed to find a way to escape, to protect himself, and to hold onto the hope that Tristian would come for him. "You think you can break me?" he spat, trying to mask the fear creeping into his voice.

Stalis smiled, his golden eyes shimmering like molten gold. "Break you? No, Tyler. I have no desire to break you. I want you to embrace what I offer. To become part of something greater. You're a wolf of the Baxtrail Pack, after all. Your loyalty could be invaluable."

"Loyalty to you?" Tyler scoffed. "You're insane if you think I'd ever side with you."

"Perhaps," Stalis said, shrugging nonchalantly. "But I also believe that the allure of power is something you'll find difficult to resist. I can show you the world as you've never imagined it. Strength, freedom, respect. All within your grasp."

"And at what cost?" Tyler countered, narrowing his eyes. "My freedom? My humanity?"

Stalis leaned in closer, a devilish grin playing at his lips. "Not your humanity, dear wolf, but rather the chains that bind you to your former life. It's a choice, Tyler. I can offer you a taste of true power, but it comes with sacrifices. You'll need to decide what you're willing to give up."

"I'd rather die than be anything of yours," Tyler shot back, the conviction in his voice ringing defiantly through the opulent room.

In an instant, the atmosphere shifted. Stalis's expression darkened, the playful glimmer in his eyes replaced by a cold, calculating intensity. "Die?" he repeated, his voice low and dangerous, like the rumble of distant thunder. "You really think I would allow such a thing? Your life is not yours to throw away, wolf. You are here for a reason, and I will not let you squander that."

Tyler felt a chill race down his spine, the threat in Stalis's tone unmistakable. The fairy prince stepped closer, his presence now suffocating, an aura of menace swirling around him. "You might wish for death, but know this: I can make your existence a living hell. You will obey, or you will suffer the consequences."

Tyler swallowed hard, fighting to maintain his defiance even as fear crept into his chest. "You can't control me."

Stalis leaned in, his golden eyes blazing with a fierce light. "Oh, but I can. And I will. You will come to understand that resistance is not just futile; it is downright foolish." His voice dropped to a near whisper, laden with a sinister promise. "I can make your dreams a nightmare, Tyler. You'd do well to remember that."

Stalis straightened, his demeanor shifting back to that of a charismatic ruler, though the underlying threat lingered like a shadow. "Take your time to adjust. You're free to explore the palace, but I suggest you don't wander too far. There are consequences for disobedience." His smile returned, but it no longer held the warmth of charm—it was a warning.

As Stalis glided toward the door, Tyler's heart raced, a whirlwind of dread and determination flooding his veins. He needed to find a way to escape, to warn Tristian, and to resist the temptation of what Stalis offered. But deep down, he felt the pull of the Fae realm—a dangerous allure that threatened to consume him whole.

With a final glance over his shoulder, Stalis disappeared through the door, leaving Tyler alone in the lavish chamber. He took a deep breath, trying to steady himself. This was not just about survival; it was about fighting back against the darkness that threatened to engulf him.

After Stalis left, Tyler took a moment to collect himself, the weight of the situation pressing heavily on his shoulders. He glanced around the luxurious chamber, noting the intricate details of the decor—the shimmering walls, the opulent furnishings—but none of it mattered. He needed to find a way out.

Determined, Tyler pushed the heavy door open and stepped into the dimly lit hallway. The palace was a maze of corridors and rooms, each more lavish than the last. Intricate murals adorned the walls, depicting scenes of Fae celebrations and battles, the air thick with the scent of magic and mystery.

As he wandered, the grandeur of the palace felt increasingly oppressive. Tyler could feel eyes watching him from the shadows, and every sound echoed through the halls, amplifying his unease. He needed a distraction—a way to keep his mind off Stalis's threat and the precariousness of his situation.

Eventually, Tyler stumbled upon a large wooden door that stood slightly ajar. Curiosity piqued, he pushed it open and stepped inside. The room was bright and warm, filled with the enticing aromas of spices and freshly baked bread.

In the center of the kitchen stood a woman, her back to him as she stirred a bubbling pot over an open flame. Her long, dark hair cascaded down her back, and she wore a simple but elegant dress that seemed to flow with the gentle movements of her body. The rhythmic clattering of utensils filled the space, creating a comforting atmosphere.

"Hello?" Tyler called out, a mix of hope and caution in his voice.

The woman turned, her eyes wide with surprise before settling into a welcoming smile. "Oh! You must be the new guest," she said, wiping her hands on a towel. "I'm Crystal. It's not often we have a wolf in the palace."

"Yeah, well, it's not often I'm kidnapped either," Tyler replied, crossing his arms defensively.

Crystal chuckled softly, her warmth contrasting with the tension that filled the air. "Fair enough. But you might find this place isn't all bad, especially if you're hungry." She gestured to the pot. "I'm making a stew. Would you like some?"

Tyler's stomach growled in response, a reminder of how long it had been since he'd eaten. "I didn't realize how starving I was," he admitted, a hint of embarrassment creeping into his voice.

"Come, sit!" Crystal said, motioning to a wooden table set with an array of ingredients and fresh bread. "I can make you a bowl. It's not fancy, but it'll fill you up."

Hesitating for just a moment, Tyler approached the table, the tantalizing aroma of the stew drawing him in. "Thanks, I appreciate it."

As Crystal ladled the steaming stew into a bowl, Tyler couldn't help but observe her closely. "You don't look like a fairy," he remarked, furrowing his brow.

Crystal paused, looking at him with curiosity. "That's because I'm not a fairy. I'm human."

Tyler blinked in surprise. "How did you end up in the Fire Court, then?"

Crystal's expression shifted slightly, a hint of sadness flickering in her eyes. "It's a long story. I was taken from my home by a group of Fae during a raid. They brought me here, and I found myself stuck in this court, doing what I can to survive. I cook for the palace now."

"Isn't it dangerous?" Tyler asked, intrigued and alarmed. "I mean, being in a place like this?"

Crystal smiled softly, shaking her head. "Not as much as you might think. I'm treated very well here. Stalis is really good to me and to the people who serve under him. He ensures that we're comfortable and taken care of. He may have his whims, but he values loyalty and hard work."

Tyler frowned, skeptical. "He seems... intense. How can you trust him?"

"He can be intense," she admitted, "but it's not all bad. I've seen him protect those he cares about, and I'm one of them. He has a strange sense of honor about him. It's hard to explain."

Tyler mulled over her words, surprised by her perspective. "So, you don't fear him?"

"Not in the way you might think," Crystal replied, stirring the pot with a gentle hand. "I respect him. There's a difference. You might find that your impression of him changes, too, once you see beyond the surface."

As she set the bowl of steaming stew in front of him, Tyler took a moment to absorb her words. Maybe there was more to Stalis and this realm than he had initially thought.

As Tyler took a cautious sip of the stew, savoring the rich flavors, he couldn't shake the feeling of unease that lingered in the back of his mind. He set the bowl down, looking up at Crystal with newfound determination. "What does Stalis want from me?"

Crystal paused, her expression shifting as she considered his question. "That's a complicated matter. Stalis has had his eye on you for a while."

"Why? Because I'm a werewolf?" Tyler pressed, the tension in his voice rising.

She nodded slowly, her gaze steady. "Yes, but it's more than that. You represent a unique opportunity for him—something he believes can enhance his power and influence in the Fae realm. Werewolves are rare, and your kind is seen as strong and resilient. Stalis has a fascination with strength, especially when it's tied to something he cannot easily control."

"Great," Tyler muttered, frustration creeping into his tone. "I'm just a pawn in his game."

Crystal placed a reassuring hand on his arm. "Not a pawn. An asset. There's a difference. Stalis respects strength, and he might see you as an ally rather than just a tool. But that doesn't mean he won't expect something in return."

"What kind of 'something'?" Tyler asked, unease growing in his gut.

"I can't say for certain," she replied softly. "He's unpredictable. But if you're wise, you'll keep your wits about you and find a way to navigate this situation to your advantage."

Tyler stared at his half-eaten stew, grappling with the weight of her words. He knew he had to tread carefully in this court of fire and power. "Thanks, Crystal. I appreciate your honesty."

"Just remember," she said, her voice low and serious, "this world is filled with magic and danger. Stalis may seem charming, but he's not someone to be underestimated."

Nodding, Tyler took another bite of the stew, contemplating his next move. The palace, with its grandiose beauty, felt like a gilded cage, and he was determined to find a way to escape its confines

As Tyler absorbed Crystal's words, the kitchen door swung open, and Stalis stepped inside. The atmosphere shifted immediately; Crystal fell silent, her demeanor changing from warm and inviting to cautious and reserved.

"Ah, what do we have here?" Stalis said, his voice smooth and playful as his golden eyes danced between the two of them. "Enjoying a little private chat, I see."

"Just having some stew," Tyler replied, trying to maintain his composure despite the tension that filled the room.

Stalis approached, a predatory smile playing on his lips as he moved closer to Tyler. "I see. Crystal always makes the best meals." He leaned over, glancing at the bowl before focusing on Tyler. "And how is it? Is it to your liking?"

"It's good," Tyler replied, his voice steadier than he felt.

Without warning, Stalis reached out and began to rub Tyler's shoulders, his touch surprisingly gentle yet possessive. The warmth of the prince's hands was at odds with the unease tightening in Tyler's chest. He stiffened under the unexpected contact, instinctively wanting to pull away but unsure of how to navigate the situation.

Stalis leaned in closer, his breath brushing against Tyler's ear. "You have nothing to fear from me, dear wolf. I only want to help you settle in."

Tyler swallowed hard, a chill running down his spine. "I'm fine," he managed to say, his discomfort growing. "I don't need help."

Stalis chuckled softly, as if amused by Tyler's resistance. "Oh, but I think you do. You're in a foreign land, and I am here to ensure your comfort." His fingers pressed a little harder into Tyler's shoulders, and Tyler could feel the prince's intent radiating off him.

"Let him go, Stalis," Crystal said suddenly, her voice laced with a hint of warning. "He's not a toy."

Stalis straightened, releasing Tyler but maintaining that playful smile. "Toys can be quite fun, Crystal. But I assure you, he's more than that." He turned his gaze back to Tyler, eyes glimmering with a mixture of mischief and something darker. "You'll come to understand the game we're playing here, Tyler. Just be patient."

As Stalis stepped back, the playful glint in his eyes shifted to something more serious. He leaned against the kitchen counter, arms crossed, his presence filling the space with an undeniable intensity. "But, dear Tyler, there's more I need to discuss with you."

"What now?" Tyler asked, his heart racing with unease.

"I've been considering our future together," Stalis said, his voice smooth and confident. "And I've come to a very exciting conclusion."

"Exciting?" Tyler echoed, disbelief threading through his words.

"Yes," Stalis continued, his golden eyes sparkling with a mixture of ambition and charm. "I plan to marry you."

Tyler blinked, processing the words. "What? No way. You can't be serious."

"Oh, but I am," Stalis replied, his tone unwavering. "Marrying me would make me the king of the Fire Court, and you would become my alpha. Together, we would form a bond that would outrank all the other courts."

Tyler's stomach twisted at the implications. "You want to use me as a pawn in your game."

"Not a pawn," Stalis insisted, stepping closer once again. "An ally, a partner. Imagine what we could accomplish together. You possess strength and resilience that I admire. The wolves and Fae united under one rule would be unstoppable."

"I'm not interested in ruling anything, especially not with you," Tyler shot back, his voice rising. "This isn't some fairytale."

Stalis tilted his head, unfazed by Tyler's resistance. "Life is rarely a fairytale, Tyler, but that doesn't mean it can't be extraordinary. You have the chance to change the course of the Fae realm, to create a legacy. All I ask is for your trust."

"Trust you?" Tyler scoffed, shaking his head. "You've taken me from my home and thrust me into this mess. How can I trust you?"

"Because I'm offering you a position of power," Stalis replied, his tone firm. "You have the ability to shape the future of the Fae realm alongside me. Don't you see? This is more than just a marriage; it's a chance to forge a new destiny."

Tyler's mind raced, the weight of Stalis's words pressing down on him. The idea of power, of forming alliances, tempted him, but he couldn't shake the feeling that he was being cornered into a decision he wasn't ready to make.

"I need time to think," Tyler said finally, his voice steadier than he felt.

"Of course," Stalis said with a smile that didn't quite reach his eyes. "Take all the time you need. Just remember, opportunities like this don't come often. The choice will ultimately be yours, but I will be waiting."

With that, Stalis stepped back, leaving the weight of his words lingering in the air. The kitchen felt charged, and Tyler could sense the gravity of the situation he found himself in.

Crystal remained quiet, her expression a mix of concern and curiosity. "What are you going to do?"

"I don't know," Tyler admitted, frustration simmering beneath the surface. "But I'm not ready to be anyone's Alpha."

Fire and Water

The sun hung high in the sky, illuminating the vibrant greens of the forest as Tristian followed Aelith down a narrow, winding path. The air was thick with the scent of moss and wildflowers, a stark contrast to the heaviness in Tristian's heart. He glanced at Aelith, who moved with an ease that suggested familiarity with the terrain.

"Why can't we just teleport to the Fire Court?" Tristian asked, frustration creeping into his voice.

Aelith shook his head, a hint of a smile playing at his lips. "Teleporting in the Fae realm doesn't work the same way it does elsewhere. The realm is ever-changing, its landscapes shifting in ways you can't always predict. It's like trying to navigate a river that keeps altering its course."

Tristian frowned, not entirely satisfied with that answer. "But it seems so inefficient to walk when we could get there much faster."

Aelith's gaze grew serious as he continued. "Efficiency isn't always the priority in our world. The journey itself holds value. Each step teaches us something new, reveals hidden truths about the realm—and about ourselves."

Tristian considered this for a moment, letting the words sink in. "You sound like you've given this a lot of thought."

"I have," Aelith replied. "Growing up in the Water Court, I learned to appreciate the subtleties of our magic. It's not just about power; it's about understanding the currents that flow around us and within us. Our abilities are tied to the essence of water—fluid, adaptable, sometimes tumultuous."

"What powers do you have?" Tristian asked, genuine curiosity surfacing. "What does it mean to be part of the Water Court?"

Aelith's eyes sparkled with enthusiasm. "We control the tides, summon rain, and can even communicate with the aquatic creatures of our realm. My magic allows me to manipulate water in all its forms—ice, vapor, liquid. But it goes deeper than that. It's about connection and harmony. We protect the waterways, ensuring that life thrives. It's a profound responsibility."

"That sounds incredible," Tristian said, admiration creeping into his voice. "But what about you personally? Do you ever feel confined by those duties?"

Aelith paused, contemplating the question. "At times, yes. There's a yearning for freedom, to explore beyond the borders of the Water Court. But every time I step away, I feel the pull of my home—the need to protect it, to uphold the balance. It's a constant struggle between duty and desire."

Tristian nodded, relating to Aelith's internal conflict. "And now you're risking it all to help me rescue Tyler. That takes courage."

"It's a risk worth taking," Aelith said, a determined glint in his eye. "Tyler's safety is paramount, and together, we can navigate this volatile world. We must be prepared for Stalis and his games. He's cunning and will exploit any weakness he can find."

Tristian swallowed hard, the weight of their mission settling heavily on his shoulders. "Do you think we can really outsmart him?"

Aelith's smile returned, more confident this time. "With our combined strength, absolutely. The essence of our magic flows together; it can be a force to reckon with. We just have to stay true to our purpose and not lose sight of why we're here."

As they continued along the path, the forest seemed to resonate with their determination, each step drawing them closer to their goal. Tristian felt a sense of camaraderie forming with Aelith, the bond of their shared journey strengthening with every word exchanged.

As they made their way through the winding forest path, Aelith glanced back at Tristian, a hint of curiosity sparking in his gaze. Breaking the quiet that hung between them, he asked, "So, why did you make a deal with Stalis anyway?"

Tristian's steps slowed, and he looked down, his expression clouded. "W ell... Tyler and I were looking for the Stone of Ohara," he said, his voice quiet but steady. "But when we got close, Stalis appeared. He wouldn't let us pass and said he'd only allow it if I..." He trailed off, frustration in the line of his jaw.

Aelith's brows lifted slightly. "Ah, I see," he replied, his voice carrying a note of understanding. He continued walking, letting Tristian's words sink in, then added, "For all we know, the stone may not even be in the Grove anymore. No creature has seen it in decades—maybe even centuries."

Tristian exhaled sharply and came to a stop, hands on his knees as he caught his breath. He cast a tired glance at Aelith. "It feels like we're searching for a ghost."

Aelith stopped too, looking back at him with a thoughtful expression. "Well... no earthly creature," he murmured, a glimmer of something unreadable in his eyes.

Tristian's head snapped up. "What do you mean?" he asked, his voice edged with new interest.

Aelith's gaze held a knowing gleam. "The moonstone, or the Stone of Ohara as you call it, has been in the Fae realm for years, it hasn't been in the Grove for a long time. It's held within the Water Court," he said softly.

Tristian blinked, the realization settling in slowly. "So all this time, the stone was out of reach?"

"Not exactly," Aelith replied, his tone carrying a warning. "The Water Court has protected it, but no one can take it without proving themselves worthy. The stone chooses who may wield its power. Even we don't attempt to use it lightly." He paused, meeting Tristian's gaze. "If Stalis knew where it was, he'd move heaven and earth to claim it."

Tristian swallowed hard, the weight of Aelith's words adding a new urgency to his mission. "So, the stone isn't just a legend. And if I could somehow gain access to it..." He looked away, mind racing with possibilities.

Aelith nodded, his face sober. "Then you'd have a way to stand against Stalis—a weapon that might even turn the tide of power in the courts. But it's not something to take lightly. The stone responds to purpose, not mere strength. It requires an unwavering heart." He reached out, resting a hand on Tristian's shoulder. "Be careful what you ask for, Tristian. The stone's gifts come at a price."

Tristian's eyes held a newfound fire as he met Aelith's gaze, his voice filled with resolve. "I'll do whatever it takes to get Tyler back. And if that means proving myself to the stone, so be it."

"Would you be able to help me get to the stone Aelith?" Tristian asked as he stared at the handsome Fae.

Aelith paused, considering Tristian's question. The forest was silent around them, the only sound was the rustle of leaves in the breeze as he seemed to weigh his answer. Finally, he met Tristian's gaze, his expression serious.

"It's not that simple," Aelith said quietly. "The stone is bound by layers of enchantment, protections that only those with Water Court lineage can even begin to break through." He crossed his arms, his face thoughtful. "But if you're truly committed to this path, then... yes, I can help you try."

Tristian felt a flicker of hope. "What do we have to do?"

Aelith's gaze turned to the horizon, where the faint shimmer of water glinted through the trees. "First, we'll need to gain the blessing of my court. No one touches the stone without permission—not even me. And the elders don't easily grant it."

Tristian's shoulders tensed at the mention of more obstacles. "So, what? We just ask them and hope they agree?"

"Not exactly," Aelith replied, a wry smile tugging at his lips. "You'll have to prove yourself worthy. And trust me, the Water Court's tests are not to be taken lightly. They can see through to the heart of your intentions, and they'll challenge every ounce of your resolve."

Tristian swallowed, his determination unshaken. "If that's what it takes, then I'll face whatever trials they set. For Tyler."

Aelith's expression softened, a hint of admiration in his eyes. "Then I'll guide you as far as I can. But remember, Tristian: once we begin, there's no turning back. The Water Court may be merciful, but the stone... it isn't."

Tristian nodded, his jaw set with resolve. "Then let's get started."

Tristian paused, his gaze drifting toward the distant horizon where the ominous spires of the Fire Court's castle pierced the sky, flickering with a faint, otherworldly glow. The castle loomed like a dark promise, a constant reminder of the danger Tyler faced. Tristian's jaw tightened as he took in the sight, dread pooling in his stomach.

He looked back at Aelith, who watched him with a calm, knowing expression. Determination simmered in Tristian's eyes, the weight of his choice pressing down on him. He knew the risks of pursuing the moonstone, knew the trials it would demand of him—but he also knew that this might be his only real chance to save Tyler.

"If the stone is our best shot," he said quietly. His voice was steady, but his fingers curled into fists at his sides, bracing for the unknown ahead.

Aelith's gaze softened, and he nodded. "Then let's keep moving. The path to the Water Court isn't as far as it seems."

With a last, resolute glance at the distant castle, Tristian turned back to the path, ready to face whatever awaited him.

***

Tyler sat cross-legged on the plush rug of his room, a stack of ancient books scattered around him. The ornate bindings and faded, intricate script hinted at the age and mystery within each volume. He ran his fingers over the text, trying to decipher the flowery language and odd symbols that made up the bulk of Fae knowledge. Yet despite his best efforts, none of the passages offered a clue about his situation or Stalis's true intentions on how he would use Tyler to rule the Fae.

The door creaked open, and Tyler looked up, his eyes narrowing as Stalis entered, moving with a grace that seemed almost too smooth, too calculated. Stalis's usual air of command was softened now, replaced by a strangely warm, polite demeanor. He smiled as he crossed the room, his eyes fixed on Tyler with a look of subtle amusement.

"Finding anything interesting?" Stalis asked, gesturing at the books with a casual wave.

Tyler straightened, setting a particularly dusty tome aside. "Just... trying to make sense of all this." His tone was neutral, cautious.

Stalis's eyes sparkled with a look of encouragement. "It's good to see you're so curious. The history of the Fae is a fascinating study—especially for someone who might soon have a stake in it." He took a few steps closer, glancing over the book Tyler had just put down.

Tyler's brow furrowed. "A stake in it? That's not exactly why I'm here, is it?"

Stalis chuckled softly, his tone gentle. "I suppose not directly, no. But knowledge of our world, our customs... it can be an advantage. After all, your role here could be more significant than you realize."

Tyler felt a chill run down his spine at the implication, though Stalis's words were as polite and measured as ever. "I'm... just trying to understand what you want with me."

Stalis paused, meeting Tyler's gaze with surprising openness. "To have a partner who understands both our worlds, who can stand beside me with insight, strength, and resilience. That is what I wish for."

Tyler's eyes narrowed slightly, reading between the lines. But Stalis just smiled, polite and patient, as if he could wait as long as it took for Tyler to grasp his meaning.

Tyler's gaze hardened, his fingers tightening around the spine of the book in his lap as he met Stalis's steady, expectant gaze.

"I have a bond to someone already," he said firmly, his voice unwavering. "And it isn't you."

Stalis's expression barely shifted, but a flicker of something—disappointment? Amusement?—glinted in his eyes. He tilted his head, regarding Tyler with a mixture of curiosity and mild reproach, as though Tyler had merely misinterpreted a well-intentioned gesture.

"Ah," Stalis murmured, his voice soft and almost sympathetic. "You mean Tristian, don't you? How sweet." He stepped closer, his tone still gentle but with a hint of steel. "But you'll find that the bond you speak of is fragile in the face of what I can offer you. Here, you'd hold power beyond anything you've known."

Tyler straightened, refusing to break eye contact. "I don't want your power. I want my freedom—and to be with Tristian."

Stalis's smile didn't waver, but his eyes grew darker, calculating. "Freedom can be such a fleeting thing, Tyler. Especially here. But I'm a reasonable host," he said, reaching out to trace the spine of a nearby book, as if the subject of their conversation were casual, inconsequential. "Perhaps, in time, you'll come to understand the true value of what I offer."

Tyler's jaw clenched, the weight of his defiance heavy yet resolute. "I doubt it."

Stalis took a step closer, his movements smooth and deliberate, as though he were choreographed to draw Tyler in. The air between them thickened, charged with an intensity that made Tyler's skin prickle. Stalis leaned slightly forward, his voice dropping to a husky murmur that felt like a caress.

"You're young, Tyler," he said, his gaze locking onto Tyler's with a predatory glint. "And I can see the depth of your feelings for Tristian. But love can be a blinding thing. It can trap you when you least expect it."

He closed the distance further, now so close that Tyler could see the subtle nuances in his expression, the way his lips curved into a seductive smile. "What I offer isn't just power; it's freedom from that trap. Imagine the possibilities of being with someone who truly understands you, who can elevate you to heights you never thought possible."

Tyler swallowed hard, caught off guard by the intimacy of Stalis' presence. "I'm not interested in what you're selling," he said, his voice steadier than he felt.

Stalis chuckled softly, the sound low and inviting. "You say that now, but I promise, I can show you a world where your desires are fulfilled, where you stand at my side as an equal. Isn't that worth considering?"

He leaned closer still, his breath warm against Tyler's skin, stirring a confusing mix of intrigue and repulsion within him. "Tristian may be noble, but he is bound by his own responsibilities. Can he truly give you what you crave?"

Tyler's heart raced, a mix of anger and fear rising within him. "I don't need you to tell me what I want. I know where I belong." He held his ground, even as Stalis's intensity threatened to pull him under.

Stalis's smile widened, revealing a hint of sharp teeth as his eyes glowed with a captivating light. The intensity of his gaze enveloped Tyler, and for a moment, the world around him blurred. Tyler felt an intoxicating wave of bliss wash over him, a warmth that spread through his body, igniting a thrilling sense of arousal he couldn't quite suppress.

"As prince of the Fire Court," Stalis murmured, his voice low and sultry, "my powers come from heat, war, destruction, and—yes—sexuality. I could make you love me, Tyler."

The words hung in the air, wrapping around Tyler like a silken thread, tugging at his resolve. He found himself teetering on the edge of surrender, entranced by the fire that flickered in Stalis's eyes. The bliss intensified, merging with an undeniable attraction that threatened to overwhelm his senses.

"You could have everything you desire," Stalis continued, his voice a seductive whisper, drawing even closer. "No more pain, no more worry—just passion and pleasure." He tilted his head, his expression one of both temptation and challenge. "Imagine giving in to that feeling. Let me show you what it means to truly feel alive."

Tyler's heart raced, battling the conflicting emotions raging within him. He knew he should resist, but the allure of Stalis's words made it increasingly difficult. The thrill of danger and the promise of ecstasy blurred the lines of his thoughts, pulling him into a world where everything felt intoxicatingly possible.

As Stalis leaned in closer, the seductive warmth pulsing between them ignited a flicker of something deep within Tyler—a bond that tugged insistently at his heart. It was a connection that reminded him of the strength he shared with Tristian, the depth of their feelings that he had fought to preserve.

Suddenly, Tyler felt an electric jolt shoot through him, and with it, his eyes ignited with a brilliant glow, reflecting the inner battle waging within. His canines elongated, sharp and fierce, a primal instinct surging forth as he instinctively growled, breaking free from Stalis's hypnotic grasp.

"Get away from me!" Tyler snarled, his voice low and guttural, echoing with the strength of the wolf within. The warm haze dissipated, leaving behind the raw intensity of his emotions.

Stalis stepped back, his expression shifting from amusement to surprise, eyes narrowing as he regarded Tyler with newfound respect. "Interesting," he said, a hint of admiration lacing his voice. "It seems you possess more strength than I anticipated."

Tyler's heart pounded, the feral energy coursing through him reaffirming his loyalty to Tristian. He could feel the bond pulling at him, urging him to fight against the temptation that Stalis represented. "I'm not yours to control," he growled, every word filled with conviction. "My bond is with Tristian, and no amount of your power will change that."

Stalis's smile returned, but it was now tinged with something darker. "Very well, Tyler. But remember this: the heart can be swayed, and my offers still stand. I could make you feel things you never thought possible."

Tyler shot him a defiant look, the fire in his eyes unwavering. "I'll never be yours."

Stalis regarded Tyler with a mixture of intrigue and amusement, his smile never fading as he straightened, reclaiming his composure. "Ah, such fierce determination. It's refreshing, truly," he said, his voice smooth like silk, but with an underlying edge. "But know this, my dear Tyler: defiance only makes the chase more thrilling. You see, I thrive on challenges."

He took a step back, crossing his arms as he surveyed Tyler with a keen eye. "You think you can resist me? That your bond with Tristian will shield you from what I can offer? The heart is a fickle thing, easily swayed by desire, especially when it's so tightly woven with fear and uncertainty."

Stalis's gaze sharpened, his expression darkening slightly. "I'm patient, Tyler. I can wait. The deeper your feelings for Tristian grow, the more vulnerable you become to the fire I represent. And once you feel that heat, once you crave it..."

He leaned closer again, lowering his voice to a conspiratorial whisper. "You may find yourself questioning everything you thought you knew about loyalty, love, and power."

With a final, lingering look, Stalis stepped back, allowing space between them but leaving an unmistakable tension in the air. "Enjoy your books, Tyler. I'll be around to remind you of what you're missing."

As he turned to leave, Tyler felt the weight of his words settle heavily in the room, a challenge lingering in the air like a promise of the battle yet to come.

Fueled by a surge of adrenaline and fury, Tyler's instincts kicked in. The heat radiating from Stalis only intensified his growing frustration, and before he could think twice, he lunged forward, teeth bared, a low growl rumbling deep in his chest.

"Get away from me!" Tyler roared, the primal essence of the wolf overtaking him as he charged toward Stalis, aiming to shove him back. The space between them shrank in an instant, the air thick with tension and defiance.

Stalis, taken aback by Tyler's sudden aggression, reacted swiftly. With a flick of his wrist, he conjured a wall of flames that sprang up between them, flickering and dancing with a ferocious energy. The heat enveloped Tyler, making the air shimmer and distort, but he was undeterred.

"Is that all you've got?" Stalis taunted, a smirk playing on his lips as he stepped back, clearly amused by Tyler's attempt. "You'll need more than bravado to challenge the prince of the Fire Court."

Tyler's determination only grew stronger. Ignoring the flames that licked at him, he pushed through the heat, focusing on the bond he shared with

Tristian. "I won't let you manipulate me!" he shouted, feeling the power of the wolf within him rising to the surface.

With a fierce roar, he dove toward the barrier of flames, ready to break through. But just as he reached the wall, Stalis raised his hand, and the fire swirled violently, creating a barrier that crackled with energy.

"Patience, my dear Tyler," Stalis said, his voice low and mocking, his eyes glowing with a fierce intensity. "You'll find that anger only gets you so far. You're stronger than this—use it wisely."

Tyler skidded to a halt, snarling as he faced the flames. The heat was overwhelming, but the fire inside him burned even hotter. "I won't be your pawn, Stalis!" he growled, his eyes narrowing.

Stalis chuckled, the sound echoing in the charged air. "Then let's see how long you can hold on to that resolve. I do love a good game." With that, he snapped his fingers, and the flames dissipated, leaving Tyler standing alone, heart pounding, the tension between them electric.

Just as the last remnants of heat faded, Tyler felt the bond he shared with Tristian tugging deep within him, a tether he couldn't ignore. His eyes glowed momentarily, and his canines elongated as the wolf within him fought against Stalis's influence. A growl escaped his lips, raw and primal, breaking him out of the trance Stalis had tried to impose.

"Now, that's the spirit," Stalis said, amusement dancing in his eyes as he stepped closer, not deterred by Tyler's display of resistance. "I was beginning to think you'd surrender."

Tyler glared at him, breathing heavily, the feral side of him simmering just beneath the surface. "I'll never give in to you," he snarled, ready to fight with every ounce of strength he had.

Stalis tilted his head, a predatory smile spreading across his face. "Very well, Tyler. But know this: resistance only makes it more fun. I can wait as long as it takes."

Just as Stalis turned to leave, he reached out and seized the magical chain made of shimmering energy that connected him to Tyler. In an instant, the chain pulled tight, yanking Tyler down to his knees. The sudden force knocked the breath from him, and he found himself looking up at Stalis, who hovered over him like a predator sizing up its prey.

"Just remember, Tristian is the reason you are here in the first place," Stalis said, his voice low and smooth, laced with an undercurrent of menace. "You are bound to me by the deal he made. I am giving you free will, Tyler—don't make me itch to take it away."

Tyler's heart raced as he gazed up at Stalis, fury and defiance swirling within him. The glow in Stalis's eyes flickered with a dangerous light, and the air around them crackled with tension. "You can't control me," he growled, trying to summon the strength to break free from the energy binding him.

Stalis merely smiled, the corners of his lips curling in amusement. "We'll see about that," he said, releasing the chain but leaving a lingering warmth on Tyler's skin, a reminder of his power. With one last, lingering look, he turned and walked away, leaving Tyler kneeling, heart pounding, every instinct screaming to fight back against the looming threat.

Shadows Dancing

Tyler sat alone in his room, the dim light casting shadows that twisted across the walls like echoes of his thoughts. Ever since Stalis had left him, that strange, lingering warmth seemed to hover in the air, making him feel as though he were never truly alone. It was as if the Fire Court itself was alive, every flicker of flame watching, whispering, and waiting.

Just as he tried to shake the feeling, a subtle warmth began pulsing through his veins—an unsettling, unnatural heat that wasn't his own. It was faint at first, almost a whisper, but it grew, filling his mind with images that felt too vivid to ignore. The room faded around him, replaced by a scene that gripped his heart with an icy dread.

He saw Tristian, his gaze softened with a smile he reserved only for Tyler...except it wasn't directed at him. Standing close to Tristian was another man—dark-haired, tall, with an easy charm. The stranger's hand brushed Tristian's shoulder in a familiar way, and Tristian's eyes lit up, something tender in the way he laughed at whatever the man had said.

Tyler's pulse quickened, and he felt his fists clench as the image deepened, sharpening with painful clarity. The scene changed. Now Tristian and the stranger were talking under a starlit sky, Tristian leaning close as if he were sharing a secret, his hand lingering on the other man's arm. There was a glint of something else in Tristian's eyes, something Tyler hadn't seen before—a glimmer of peace, even happiness.

The vision rippled with another jolt of warmth, like a fevered pulse, as Stalis's voice echoed around him.

"Does it surprise you?" Stalis's voice was a soft murmur in his ear. "Humans are...vulnerable. They can't live their lives wrapped in waiting and longing for something they can't have."

Tyler growled, shaking his head as he tried to break free from the vision's hold. "This isn't real. He would never...he wouldn't..."

"Wouldn't he?" Stalis's voice took on an almost sympathetic tone, his presence now close beside Tyler. "He thinks you're lost, taken from him. How long do you think he'll mourn you before he seeks comfort elsewhere?"

The room seemed to dissolve, and now Tyler found himself in an entirely different place: an unfamiliar forest bathed in moonlight, an eerie, peaceful calm settling over the scene. Tristian walked beneath the trees, hand in hand with the same stranger, both of them sharing quiet smiles as they spoke in hushed tones, their laughter drifting through the trees like a song.

Tyler's heart ached, a flash of jealousy and helplessness roaring to life within him, threatening to choke him with its intensity. He felt the wolf within him stir, a fierce, protective instinct begging to be unleashed. "He wouldn't give up on me," he whispered, his voice barely audible. "Not after everyt hing..."

"Ah, but even the strongest bonds can break," Stalis whispered, his tone laced with gentle menace. "And even the truest hearts can falter. Love, you'll learn, can fade as quickly as it blooms."

Tyler fought to shake off the vision, trying to bring himself back to reality, but the warmth from Stalis's spell persisted, wrapping around him like chains. Each image seared into his mind, a slow, relentless attack on his loyalty, his heart. He could feel the doubt creeping in, clawing at him like shadows. What if Tristian...what if he really did...?

The warmth suddenly vanished, the vision fading into darkness, leaving Tyler kneeling, alone in his room, his heart racing and his breaths shallow. He gritted his teeth, fists clenched so tightly his knuckles turned white. No. Stalis would not break him. Not this way.

The sound of quiet laughter filled the room, drawing his gaze upward. Stalis had appeared in the doorway, leaning against the frame with an almost pitying smile on his face.

"So quick to dismiss it?" Stalis asked, tilting his head as he surveyed Tyler's shaken expression. "All I did was show you possibilities. Seeds of doubt already live within you, Tyler. All I need to do is water them."

Tyler looked up, eyes blazing with defiance, but a flicker of uncertainty lingered. "You won't win. I know what's real."

Stalis's smile grew, dark and knowing. "Perhaps, but the heart is a fragile thing, my dear wolf. Even the fiercest of loyalties can crumble when faced with enough fire."

With a final glance, Stalis turned and disappeared into the shadows, leaving Tyler alone in the silence, his heart heavy with both rage and fear.

***

Tristian's breath came in shallow puffs as he pushed through the forest undergrowth, damp moss and pine scenting the crisp night air. Beside him, Aelith moved with an effortless grace that belied the tension rippling between them. Tristian's fingers twitched at his side, a subtle reaction to the shared apprehension that crackled in the air. The faint glow of moonlight glistened on his silvery hair, casting him in an almost ethereal light. Despite the stillness of the forest, a current of urgency crackled around them, urging them forward.

"Are you sure this is the right path?" Tristian asked, his voice barely above a whisper. He glanced over at Aelith, who, despite the quiet, looked more determined than ever. The fairy's emerald eyes glimmered with an unreadable expression as he nodded.

"I can feel it," Aelith replied, his voice as fluid and cool as the water he commanded. "The gem's power calls to the essence of the Water Court. We're close."

Tristian nodded, though unease gnawed at the edges of his mind. It had felt like weeks since they'd embarked on their journey, driven by the desperate hope that the gem would be the key to ending the conflict between the courts. Yet, each step brought new uncertainties. The memory of Tyler's warm smile haunted him, a reminder of why he had to succeed—and why failure was not an option.

The silence stretched between them as they pressed on, broken only by the whisper of leaves and the distant sound of trickling water. Tristian's heartbeat quickened, the weight of their mission pressing against his chest like a vice. Doubt clawed at the edges of his mind, yet he forced himself to stay focused, drawing strength from the determination that had carried them this far. Aelith's movements suddenly stilled, his wings twitching as his eyes narrowed, tension coiling through his body.

"Someone's here," he said, a sharp edge in his tone. Tristian followed Aelith's gaze and saw the faintest shimmer, as though the air itself had rippled. He barely had time to react before a figure emerged from the shadows, their presence both commanding and cold.

"Aelith, you should have never left the court without permission. A prince of the Water Court abandoning his post—unthinkable." Aelith's jaw tightened, a flicker of guilt and defiance crossing his features as he met the man's gaze. The weight of his unspoken secrets pressed heavily on him, but he stood resolute. I was sent to bring you both back, and know this—you're going back, just more for trial than willingly." The stranger's voice was smooth, taunting. He stepped into the moonlight, revealing features both familiar and unsettling. His dark eyes glistened with a sly amusement, and a jagged scar ran across his cheek—a mark of battles hard won.

Aelith tensed, a slight tremor in the set of his jaw. Tristian's breath caught, shock flaring in his chest. A prince? Aelith had never mentioned that before.

"Caius," Aelith muttered, the name laced with a mix of anger and dread.

""Well, we were headed there anyway," Aelith said, a hint of smugness in his tone, though the tension in his stance betrayed his unease." Aelith said with a smugness to his tone. Caius's smirk deepened, his gaze flicking between Aelith and Tristian. "Headed there, were you? Without protection or the council's blessing? How naive," he drawled, stepping closer. The moonlight caught the scar on his cheek, making it appear even more severe, a testament to the battles that had shaped him.

Aelith's wings twitched, the only sign of his growing agitation. "We don't need your protection, Caius. We're more than capable of handling what lies ahead."

"It's not for your protection, Prince Aelith. You and your witch friend are going on trial."

Tristian felt the tension twist in his chest, the revelation of Aelith's true identity still simmering under his skin. How had he not known? A flood of questions crashed through him, each one sharpening the edge of his surprise and doubt. He shifted his gaze to Caius, noting the barely restrained power in his stance. "Why now, Caius? Why come after us when we're so close?" Tristian's voice was steady, but he couldn't shake the sense that they were on the precipice of something much larger than their original mission.

Caius's smile turned cold, eyes hardening as he spoke. "Because the court won't tolerate betrayal. A prince running off in pursuit of something so silly as a broken wing? It's reckless." His tone dropped, heavy with meaning. "And dangerous, mortals and witches are dangerous"

"Not to mention," Caius continued, "there are talks of things happening in the Fire Court, plans to take over us all."

Tristian's eyes narrowed as he stepped forward, determination burning in his gaze. "That's why we're going—to get permission to use the Gem Stone. It's the only way to stop this before it's too late."

Caius's eyes widened, genuine surprise breaking through his cold demeanor. "Use the Gem Stone? For personal reasons? You truly don't understand what you're meddling with."

Caught between the revelation of Aelith's heritage and the looming threat from Caius, Tristian felt the weight of their quest settle even heavier on his shoulders. His resolve, however, only hardened; the urgency of their mission couldn't be overstated, especially now with the stakes rising and new players revealing themselves.

"Understand or not, it's our only chance," Tristian argued, his voice firm despite the churn of emotions inside him. "If we don't use the Gem Stone, the conflict will escalate beyond our control. We've seen enough bloodshed, Caius. This isn't just about the courts anymore..or just my world—it's about survival."

Caius's smirk faded into a grudging respect, his posture subtly shifting as he assessed Tristian anew. "Perhaps," he conceded slowly, "but your actions could also bring unprecedented chaos. The Gem Stone's power isn't to be taken lightly, nor is it the saviour you hope for. There are consequences to wielding such force, consequences that could affect all the realms."

Aelith, who had been silently battling his own turmoil, stepped beside Tristian, his expression now one of steel. "And we're ready to face those consequences. Caius, you know as well as I do that desperate times call for desperate measures. We didn't choose this path lightly. Please just support us"

Caius's gaze hardened as he weighed their words, the shadows of the forest casting his features into stark relief. "Support you? You'd have me betray my duties based on a hope? No. If you want my silence, if you want my aid, you'll have to earn it," he declared, his voice resonant with challenge.

He stepped back, creating space between them, his movements graceful yet filled with a lethal precision. "Prove your worth, prove the depth of your resolve. Beat me in combat, and I'll consider your cause worthy. Fail, and I will take you both back in chains."

Tristian and Aelith exchanged a quick, determined glance. The sudden challenge wasn't what they had hoped for, but neither could they back down. Not now, with so much at stake. Tristian felt the surge of adrenaline, the magical energies gathering at his fingertips, ready to respond.

Aelith squared his shoulders, his wings flaring slightly. "Then we fight," he stated simply, his voice carrying a new weight. The prince of the Water Court, now revealed and standing tall beside the witch he chose to defend.

Caius nodded, a grim smile touching his lips. He raised his hands, and water from the nearby stream lifted into the air, swirling into icy shards that glimmered in the moonlight. "Prepare yourselves."

The fight erupted with the sudden ferocity of a storm. Caius unleashed a volley of ice shards, each one aimed with deadly precision. Tristian deflected them with barriers of shimmering energy, his chants weaving stronger spells as he searched for an opening. Aelith, more agile, darted forward, manipulating the moisture in the air to create daggers of water that lashed at Caius, attempting to bind and disarm.

In the tense moments of their encounter, Tristian knew they needed a decisive advantage. As Caius unleashed a flurry of icy projectiles, Tristian focused deeply, drawing upon the ambient magical forces swirling in the forest. He envisioned the intricate weavings of a spell rarely used, one that required both precision and profound magical insight—the Arcane Pulse.

With whispered incantations, Tristian extended his hands, palms facing outward toward Caius. The air around them vibrated with the build-up of energy, leaves rustling and twigs snapping under the invisible pressure. As the spell took form, Tristian's fingers traced complex sigils in the air, channeling the latent energy of the forest into a concentrated burst.

The Arcane Pulse was a spell designed to disrupt and destabilize. When released, it sent a shockwave of pure magical force radiating outward. This force was uniquely effective against other magic users; it was tuned to seek out and unravel the threads of any active spells, leaving its target disoriented and momentarily weakened.

As Tristian unleashed the spell, a visible ripple of translucent energy surged from his hands, washing over Caius like a tidal wave. The icy shards in mid-air faltered, their trajectories disrupted, some shattering into harmless frost that sprinkled to the ground. Caius, caught in the full brunt of the pulse, staggered backward. His own magical constructs dissolved, and a brief flash of vulnerability crossed his face as he struggled to maintain his footing.

The effect of the Arcane Pulse was brief but profound. It created the opening Aelith needed to move in with water whips, capturing Caius in a fluid, binding embrace. This strategic use of the Arcane Pulse not only demonstrated Tristian's tactical acumen but also his deep reservoir of magical power and control. It was a testament to his training and his connection to the elemental energies that coursed through the natural world around them.

Breathing heavily, Caius surveyed the determination in their faces, the raw power they had displayed. With a reluctant nod, he relaxed his stance, signaling defeat. "Very well. You have proven your strength, and perhaps, your right to pursue this path. I will stand with you—but remember, the risks are great, and the path is laced with danger."

As they released him, an unspoken respect settled among them. Tristian and Aelith, their resolve reinforced by victory, now faced their journey with a new ally—however tentative. Their mission had gained both legitimacy and a formidable guardian, but the true test of the Gem Stone's power remained ahead.

Good Tidings

"In the earliest days, when the moon cast its first light and the stars whispered to the night, the realms of Fae, Witches, Vampires, and Wolves existed in a rare, harmonious accord. United by their differences yet bound by their respect for each other, these creatures thrived in an age of unparalleled peace and prosperity. Understanding the fragile nature of this peace, the ancients formed a coven that transcended their individual allegiances—a circle of powerful beings determined to sustain the harmony among their peoples.In the heart of an enchanted forest, where the veils between worlds were thin, this coven forged the Gem Stone. Crafted from the essence of each realm—fae dust, witch's blood, vampire's fang, and wolf's fur—the stone radiated a power so profound, so pure, that it could unite all creatures under its glow. It was an emblem of peace, a beacon of shared power and protection.For centuries, the Gem Stone stood at the center of the Grand Council Hall, revered and guarded by those who knew its worth. But as the ages passed, the memory of discord faded, and the vigilance of the ancient creatures waned. It was during this time of complacency that tragedy struck—a tragedy born from a love forbidden.A young witch, enamored by the simplicity and beauty of a human, fell deeply in love. This love, pure yet fraught with peril, led her to commit an unthinkable act. Blinded by passion, she stole the Gem Stone under the cloak of night, intending to grant her human beloved the gift of magic, to elevate him to her magical plane.The human, intoxicated by the sudden surge of power, became a vessel of unbridled magical force. Untrained and unstable, his powers grew wild, uncontrollable, ripping through the fabric of their worlds. The balance that had been so carefully maintained by the Gem Stone shattered, sparking fear and resentment among the creatures .The Vampires felt betrayed, their trust in the unity of the realms broken. The Wolves, ever protective of the natural order, howled in despair, their cries echoing through the forests. The Fae, guardians of balance, retreated into their hidden enclaves, while the Witches, divided by their loyalties, faced a schism that threatened to destroy their very essence.War erupted—a war that would see brother turn against brother, friend against friend. The land was scarred with the battles fought over the control of the Gem Stone, each creature vying to reclaim it and restore the peace that was lost.The witch and her human lover were ultimately consumed by the very powers she sought to share, a stark reminder of the Gem Stone's might and the price of disrupting the sacred balance."Caius finished the story as he stared into the fire's flame that the three of them sat around.As the last flickers of the fire cast their glow on the trio, Caius's voice faded into the crackling sounds of the cooling embers. Tristian, still absorbing the weight of the legend, shifted his gaze from the dying fire to his companions."We know its location within the Water Court," Tristian said, his voice carrying a blend of determination and urgency. "And I need it not just to restore peace among the realms but to secure a future where Tyler and I can be together without fear."Aelith nodded, understanding the personal stakes involved for Tristian. "Then it's more than a quest for peace—it's a fight for love. That makes it even more crucial we succeed without alerting those who would use the stone for less noble purposes."Caius, observing the resolve in Tristian's eyes, leaned back slightly, the remnants of the fire illuminating his thoughtful expression. "Love has always been a powerful motivator, for better or worse. It drove the witch to steal the stone once; let us hope it guides Tristian and his pet.. more wisely."Tristian's jaw set firmly, the mention of the past only strengthening his resolve. "It will," he asserted. "Because unlike before, we understand the full consequences of wielding the Gem Stone. And I'll do whatever it takes to ensure it brings healing, not harm."The group's collective attention turned to the path ahead, the darkness of the night giving way to the first hints of dawn. The journey to the Water Court was fraught with unknowns, but Tristian's personal stake in the outcome—a chance to be with Tyler—added a layer of resolve to their mission."We should reach the Water Court by nightfall," Aelith interjected, his tone practical yet supportive. "Let's use the remaining time to prepare for any challenges we might face. Knowing the stone's power and the history you've shared, Caius, we need to be ready for anything my parents want to throw at us."With a mutual nod, they extinguished what was left of the fire and gathered their belongings. Each step they took was laden with the gravity of their quest, but also with the hope of what achieving their goals could mean—not just for the realms, but for Tristian and Tyler's future.As they moved through the forest, the light of the rising sun began to pierce through the trees, casting long shadows and bathing their path in a soft, promising light. The journey was not just a mission to retrieve an artifact; it was a step toward a dream of peace and love that Tristian was unwilling to abandon.***Tyler sat at the small, rustic kitchen table, his plate nearly empty but for a few crumbs and the remnants of a hearty meal. The warm glow of the kitchen lights and the comforting scent of roasted potatoes and herbs filled the air, creating a homely atmosphere. Crystal, always the caretaker, noticed the emptiness of his plate and moved towards him with the pot of potatoes, her smile kind."Here, you look like you could use a bit more," she said, spooning another generous helping onto his plate. The potatoes were golden and crisp, just the way he liked them."Thanks, Crystal," Tyler murmured, his thoughts distant, wandering to Tristian and the dangers he might be facing.Their light chatter about mundane daily tasks filled the kitchen until the door creaked open, ushering in a draft of cool air. Stalis stepped inside, and the atmosphere subtly shifted. The warmth of the kitchen seemed to recede slightly at his entrance. His presence always brought a tingle of tension, but today, his usual stern expression was replaced with an unsettling cheerfulness."Good evening," Stalis greeted them, his voice smooth and almost carefree. He hung his cloak by the door, a slight smile playing at the corners of his lips.Crystal paused, a frown briefly raising her brow as she placed the pot back on the stove. The change in Stalis's demeanor did not go unnoticed, and her hands tightened around the spoon. "Evening, Stalis. Did the day treat you well?" she asked, her tone polite yet cautious."Exceptionally well, thank you for asking," Stalis replied, his eyes glinting with an unspoken knowledge as he glanced from Crystal to Tyler. His smile broadened slightly, as if he harbored a secret that only added to his good mood.Tyler's fork paused halfway to his mouth, his senses sharpening. Stalis in a good mood was not a common occurrence and seldom meant something benign. "What brings you to the kitchen? You usually don't come down here this time of evening," Tyler said, trying to sound casual but his voice was tight with a mixture of curiosity and apprehension."Just wanted to see how our resident soon to be prince is holding up without his other half. It's rare to see you so... domestic," Stalis teased lightly, but his eyes scanned Tyler's face for any sign of vulnerability.Crystal exchanged a worried glance with Tyler, picking up on the undercurrents in Stalis's tone. "We manage just fine," she interjected quickly, her protective instincts flaring up. "Tyler's been a great help around here.""Is that so?" Stalis walked over to the table, pulling out a chair with a casual grace and sitting down. "Well, I must say, it's refreshing to see such... resilience. But let us not dwell on the hardships, shall we? I bring good tidings from my ventures today—things are looking up for our little enclave."Tyler and Crystal shared a look, both puzzled and on edge about what Stalis's words could imply. His good moods were rarely without consequence, and his cryptic announcement did nothing to ease the growing tension."Good tidings?" Tyler echoed, setting his fork down. "What kind of tidings? And no one says that anymore..."Stalis leaned back, his eyes half-closed as if savoring a private joke while ignoring Tyler's comment. "Oh, just some shifts in the winds, opportunities arising that could benefit us all. But let's save that for another time. Tonight, let's enjoy our evening, shall we?"His nonchalance did little to mask the undercurrents of his words, leaving Tyler and Crystal even more wary. As Stalis hummed a tune under his breath, a mix of suspicion and anticipation hung in the air, making the simple act of finishing dinner seem like a strategic pause in a much larger game.Tyler eyed Stalis warily, the unease coiling tighter in his stomach as he watched the other man's too-pleasant demeanor. "You're being weird..." he muttered, more to himself than to anyone else, though the words hung clear in the air between them.Stalis chuckled, a sound that seemed too light for the heavy atmosphere. "Oh, that's not very polite to say to your future husband," he quipped with a smirk, watching Tyler's reaction closely.The comment was like a spark to dry tinder. Tyler's face flushed with anger, and he slammed his fork down onto the plate, making Crystal jump. "I will never be your husband," Tyler snapped, his voice harsh with frustration and the pent-up stress of dealing with Stalis's manipulations.Tyler's words hung in the air, charged with defiance and disgust. But Stalis, unfazed, only smiled, his demeanor darkening with an edge of something more sinister. Instead of leaving, he stepped closer to Tyler, closing the distance with a slow, deliberate tread.As Stalis approached, Tyler's instinct was to step back, to put space between them, but his body didn't respond to his mind's urgent commands. He found himself frozen, his muscles locked in place as Stalis reached out and gently, almost tenderly, touched his face.A cold shiver ran down Tyler's spine, his eyes widening with the realization of what was happening. Stalis had him under some sort of spell, his magic ensnaring Tyler effortlessly, binding him to stillness."Oh, Tyler," Stalis murmured, his voice soft yet chilling, "there's no need for such hostility. We could be so much more to each other if you just let go of your resistance."Tyler wanted to jerk away, to shout, to do anything but stand there passively, but the spell held him tight, rendering him powerless. His heart pounded against his ribcage, panic and anger swirling within him as Stalis's thumb caressed his cheek.From the corner of his eye, Tyler saw Crystal standing by the table, her expression a mixture of fear and sorrow. She clenched her hands into fists at her sides, her body tense as if she was fighting her own battle not to intervene. But they both knew that any confrontation with Stalis could have dire consequences, especially with his magic at play.Crystal's eyes met Tyler's, her sadness mirrored in his gaze, a silent apology that she could do nothing to help him. It was a moment of profound helplessness for both of them, caught in the web of Stalis's power and intentions.Stalis leaned in closer, his breath a whisper against Tyler's ear. "Consider my words, Tyler. The world is changing, and we must adapt with it. You'll see, in time, that I can offer you more than you've ever dreamed."Finally, as abruptly as it had taken hold, the spell released Tyler, and he stumbled back, gasping for breath, his face flushed with a mix of relief and lingering fear. Stalis stepped back, his smile unfaltering, as if pleased with the demonstration of his control.As Tyler tried to compose himself, still reeling from the encounter, Crystal stood silently by the table, her presence a comforting but tense figure in the room. Her face was pinched with worry as she observed Tyler's distress. Then, closing her eyes, she focused intently. Tyler watched, puzzled, as her lips moved slightly, whispering words too soft to catch.Tyler's head suddenly filled with Crystal's voice, clear and urgent, "Kiss him. Give him what he wants and make him think you're on his side." The message echoed in his mind, startling him with its clarity and the unexpected method of delivery.Tyler blinked, his confusion evident. "How did you...?" he began, turning to face Crystal. His voice trailed off as he realized the implications. Crystal was human, or so he had thought. Humans didn't have telepathic abilities, not without some form of magical intervention.Crystal opened her eyes, meeting Tyler's stunned gaze. "I'll explain later," she lipped, her voice not even audible to avoid drawing Stalis' attention.Tyler felt a swirl of emotions—betrayal, confusion, but above all, a desperate need to cling to any strand of hope. Stalis' presence, still looming nearby, was a stark reminder of the danger he might be iin. Tyler's glance flickered between Stalis and Crystal, the weight of the decision pressing down on him.With a heavy heart and a mind clouded with doubts, Tyler turned slowly back to face

Stalis. The man's eyes were observant, calculating, missing nothing. Tyler forced a tense smile, masking his inner turmoil as best as he could."Maybe you're right, Stalis. Maybe I need to reconsider... everything," Tyler said, his voice betraying a hint of the confusion he felt but also a feigned contemplation, playing into the role Crystal had hastily thrust upon him.Stalis's smile widened slightly, sensing the shift in Tyler's stance. "That's very wise of you, Tyler. I knew you'd see reason eventually," he replied, his tone smooth and reassuring, yet with an undercurrent of victory.As Stalis approached once again, Tyler steeled himself for what he must do next, his mind racing with the implications of his actions, not only for himself but for all those entwined in this precarious game of power and deception.Tyler steadied his breathing, the weight of Crystal's telepathic advice heavy in his mind. Stalis, interpreting Tyler's hesitation as contemplation, stepped closer, a predatory smile tugging at his lips. His eyes locked onto Tyler's with an intensity that was both commanding and expectant."Sometimes, Tyler, the most profound shifts in allegiance begin with a simple act," Stalis whispered, his voice a seductive murmur that filled the space between them with a charged energy.Tyler's heart raced, and he struggled to keep his expression neutral, his mind racing through the consequences of what he was about to do. What Tristian might think. He knew the importance of convincing Stalis of his feigned submission; not just to protect himself, but to buy ti me.With a barely perceptible nod to himself, Tyler closed the distance. His movements were hesitant at first, but as he approached Stalis, he let a mask of resolve slip over his features. Stalis watched him, a flicker of surprise and delight crossing his otherwise controlled expression.Tyler reached up, his hand tentatively touching Stalis's cheek, feeling the rough stubble against his palm. The contact sparked a jolt of revulsion inside him, but he pressed it down, focusing on the act he had to perform.Leaning in, Tyler pressed his lips against Stalis', the kiss a mixture of necessity and strategy. It was brief, a mere moment that held the weight of a thousand promises and lies. As he pulled back, he searched Stalis's face for any sign of his thoughts, hoping his actions had been convincing enough.Stalis's eyes were wide, a mix of satisfaction and a new-found respect glinting within them. "Very good, Tyler. I knew there was more to you than meets the eye," he said, his voice low and pleased. His hand reached up to caress the side of Tyler's face, his touch lingering far longer than Tyler was comfortable with.Tyler fought to keep his demeanor calm, despite the turmoil raging inside him. He stepped back, putting a small but significant distance between them. "I hope this proves my... willingness to understand your perspective," Tyler said, each word measured and heavy with double meaning.Stalis nodded, a slow, deliberate motion. "Indeed, it does. And believe me, Tyler, this can change everything."As Stalis turned away, presumably to give them both a moment to process the encounter, Tyler's gaze fell on Crystal. She was watching with a pained expression, her eyes filled with both sorrow for what Tyler had just endured and a fierce determination. Tyler's action, while distasteful, had bought him an invaluable advantage, and he could only hope that it would lead to a turning point in their desperate situation.

Crystal gave him a small, supportive nod, her presence a silent promise that she was with him, no matter what lay ahead. Tyler took a deep breath, steeling himself for the next phase of their precarious plan, the taste of the kiss lingering like a bitter reminder of the sacrifice he was willing to make for their cause.Tyler watched as Stalis retreated, his steps measured and thoughtful. With Stalis momentarily out of earshot, Tyler turned his full attention to Crystal, his expression fraught with both confusion and a pressing need for answers.

"How did you do that? How did you send that message?" Tyler's voice was low, urgent, his eyes searching Crystal's for any hint of deceit. He needed to understand the full extent of what they were dealing with, especially now that he had compromised himself in such a significant way.

Crystal met his gaze, her features softening with understanding. "I know it's confusing," she began, her voice equally low to keep their conversation private. "While I am mostly human, there's a bit of witchcraft far up my family line. It's rare, but every few generations, someone is born with a small ability. It's never anything as strong as a full witch, just... echoes of that old power."

Tyler absorbed her words, the revelation adding another layer to the complex tapestry of their current predicament. "So, you have telepathy?" he asked, trying to piece together the implications."Not exactly full telepathy. I can't read minds, and I can't send detailed messages to just anyone. It's more like... sending feelings, strong impressions. It works best over short distances, and even then, only when I'm very focused," Crystal explained, her eyes flickering with a mix of reluctance and resignation. "I've mostly kept it a secret, fearing it might make me a target."

Tyler nodded slowly, processing the new information. "And you used it today because...""Because I had to," Crystal interjected firmly. "I saw no other way to communicate with you without risking Stalis overhearing. I thought it might give us an edge."

The weight of her decision, made in the spur of the moment to protect him, settled heavily on Tyler. He understood the risk she took, not just with Stalis but by revealing her secret to him. "Thank you," he said sincerely, his initial shock giving way to gratitude. "For trusting me with this, for using it to help us."Crystal smiled, a wry, tired curve of her lips. "We're in this together, Tyler. Whatever it takes to get through this, to keep you—and all of us—safe."

Tyler's respect for Crystal deepened, reinforced by her willingness to expose her hidden abilities for their cause. The path forward was fraught with danger, but knowing they were united in their efforts provided a sliver of comfort."We need to plan our next move," Tyler said, determination lining his voice as he glanced back to ensure Stalis was still out of earshot. "Now more than ever."Crystal nodded, her expression steeling with resolve. "Let's do that, I'm tired of being stuck here. Although, we need make sure we're ready for whatever comes next."Together, they began to discuss their strategy, aware that each moment brought new challenges but also opportunities to turn the tide in their favor, and bring Stalis down.